THE COMPLETE CHANSONS

Livre quatrième des chansons . . . (1591)

Other Chansons

RECENT RESEARCHES IN THE MUSIC OF THE RENAISSANCE

James Haar and Howard Mayer Brown, general editors

A-R Editions, Inc., publishes six quarterly series—

Recent Researches in the Music of the Middle Ages and Early Renaissance,
Margaret Bent, general editor;

Recent Researches in the Music of the Renaissance,
James Haar and Howard Mayer Brown, general editors;

Recent Researches in the Music of the Baroque Era,
Robert L. Marshall, general editor;

Recent Researches in the Music of the Classical Era,
Eugene K. Wolf, general editor;

Recent Researches in the Music of the Nineteenth and Early Twentieth Centuries,
Rufus Hallmark, general editor;

Recent Researches in American Music,
H. Wiley Hitchcock, general editor—

which make public music that is being brought to light
in the course of current musicological research.

Each volume in the *Recent Researches* is devoted
to works by a single composer or to a single genre of composition,
chosen because of its potential interest to scholars and performers,
and prepared for publication according to the standards that govern
the making of all reliable historical editions.

Subscribers to this series, as well as patrons of subscribing institutions,
are invited to apply for information about the "Copyright-Sharing Policy"
of A-R Editions, Inc., under which the contents of this volume
may be reproduced free of charge for study or performance.

Correspondence should be addressed:

A-R EDITIONS, INC.
315 West Gorham Street
Madison, Wisconsin 53703

RECENT RESEARCHES IN THE MUSIC OF THE RENAISSANCE • VOLUMES LXIII and LXIV

André Pevernage

THE COMPLETE CHANSONS

Livre quatrième
des chansons . . . (1591)
Other Chansons

Edited by Gerald R. Hoekstra

A-R EDITIONS, INC. • MADISON

ANDRE PEVERNAGE
THE COMPLETE CHANSONS

Edited by Gerald R. Hoekstra

Recent Researches in the Music of the Renaissance

Volume LX	*Chansons . . . Livre premiere . . .* (1589)
Volume LXI	*Livre second des chansons . . .* (1590)
Volume LXII	*Livre troisième des chansons . . .* (1590)
Volume LXIII	*Livre quatrième des chansons . . .* (1591) (beginning)
Volume LXIV	*Livre quatrième des chansons . . .* (1591) (conclusion) Other Chansons

Library of Congress Cataloging in Publication Data:

Pevernage, André, 1542 or 3–1591.
[Chansons. Selections]
Livre quatrième des chansons—(1591) ; Other chansons.

(The complete chansons / André Pevernage ; [v. 4])

(Recent researches in the music of the Renaissance, ISSN 0486-123X ; v. 63–64)

For 6–8 voices.
French secular or Latin sacred words.
Livre quatrième des chansons edited from the 1st ed. published: Antwerp : Impriemerie plantinienne, 1591.
Words also printed as text with English translations: p.
Includes bibliographical references.
"Un jour l'amant et l'amie / Orlando" : p.
1. Chansons, Polyphonic. I. Hoekstra, Gerald R. II. Pevernage, André, 1542 or 3–1591. Chansons, livre 4e. 1983 III. Series: Pevernage, André, 1542 or 3–1591. Chansons ; v. 4. IV. Series: Recent researches in the music of the Renaissance ; v. 63–64.
M2.R2384 vol. 63–64 [M1579] 83-9964
ISBN 0-89579-183-8 (set)
ISBN 0-89579-190-0 (v. 4)

Contents

Other Chansons

Introduction

Livre quatrième des chansons . . . (1591)

When J. Gheesdalius paid tribute to André Pevernage in his poem "In musicam Andreae Pevernagii," which appears at the end of the latter's *Livre quatrième des chansons*, he concluded with the statement: "At his death Music will fall still and silent among the Belgians." Even allowing for a certain degree of hyperbole customary in such a poem, Gheesdalius's words reveal the high regard in which Pevernage was held by his countrymen. Since the composer died just a few months after the poem was published, the words also turned out to be, in a sense, prophetic: Pevernage was one of the last of a line of prominent composers working in Antwerp.

Four books devoted to the chansons of André Pevernage were issued between 1589 and 1591 by the firm of Christopher Plantin. They contain the composer's entire known output in the genre, except for four chansons published in anthologies of the time. These four chansons include three *a 4* in *Le Rossignol musical* (Phalèse, 1597) and one *a 2* in three *parties*[1] in *Bicinia, sive cantiones* (Phalèse and Bellère, 1590). All of Pevernage's chansons are edited in the present Recent Researches in the Music of the Renaissance series (RRRen vols. LX–LXIV). This volume (RRRen LXIII–LXIV) contains all of the chansons of Book IV and also the additional pieces from *Le Rossignol musical* and *Bicinia, sive cantiones*, and this Introduction deals specifically with these pieces alone. For information of a more general nature concerning the composer and his music, see the Preface in RRRen volume LX.[2]

Whereas the first three books consist of five-voice chansons, *Livre quatrième* offers chansons for six, seven, and eight voices. Its title page (see Plate I) attributes the printing to "l'Imprimerie Plantinienne, Chez la Vefve, & Jean Mourentorf." Jean Mourentorf (or Moretus) had taken over the firm's operations in Antwerp after Plantin's death in 1589.[3] The format and high quality of the printing shows no break with the tradition evidenced in the earlier volumes, however.

The *Livre quatrième des chansons* is dedicated to the burgomasters and senators of Antwerp (see Plate II). The dedication reads:

> To the noble, prudent, and virtuous Lords Edward van der Dilft, Charles Malineus, Burgomasters, and other Senators of the renowned city of Antwerp:
>
> My Lords, having for many years experienced the good affections, benevolences and favor of your Lordships, both in particulars and generally, and after having brought to light during the past year three Books of similar Music, I have wanted to reserve this, my fourth, which is different from the preceding ones, to conclude my publications, and to present it before your Lordships, as before an assembly of one of the most praiseworthy and renowned Republics of all Europe. I beseech you not to pay so much attention to the value of the gift as to the promptness and ardor which I have in serving you, humbly and as a loyal and grateful beneficiary of your generosity. I assure your Lordships that if it pleases you to receive favorably this my little work, and to put it under your protection and defense, this will encourage me (and perhaps some other practitioners of the said science) to produce some other works of greater weight in celebration of this our fatherland. I pray in this respect that the Creator, My Lords (after my very humble and affectionate commendations to your good graces) may bestow upon you increasing honors and fulfillment of your noble and virtuous desires. Antwerp, the 12th of January, 1591.
>
> Your very humble and affectionate servant
> André Pevernage

The dedicatory aspect of the volume continues in the opening pages of music with the setting in three *parties* (nos. 1–3) of selected strophes from Jan van der Noot's *Louange de la ville d'Anvers*. All six strophes of van der Noot's *Louange* appear on the penultimate page of Pevernage's volume (see Plate IV). The strophes set by Pevernage—the first, second, and fifth—call on Clio, the muse of history, to join in lauding, respectively, the virtues of the city, its government, and its beautiful women. The third, fourth, and sixth strophes of van der Noot's poem sing the praises of the merchants, the financial institutions, and the city that "nourishes good spirits and has no equal."[4] It is not unlikely that van der

Noot's poem and Pevernage's musical setting were intended for some civic celebration, although no specific event can be cited. They may, of course, have been written simply to grace a volume that was dedicated to the city fathers. According to the city's records, Pevernage's tribute did not go unrewarded. The composer was awarded a stipend as a gesture of gratitude:

> Andries Pevernage, singing master of Our Lady Church, here 50 lb. for an honorarium and payment for honoring this city with a certain music book of six, seven, and eight parts, of which he has also presented a richly bound copy to the city.[5]

A note in the margin of the records informs us that the copy was placed in "the inventory of the collection of the library of this city."[6]

The six partbooks of *Livre quatrième* are labeled Superius, Contratenor, Tenor, Bassus, Quinta, and Sexta. The Sexta functions in all of the six-voice pieces as an additional superius. The range of the Quinta varies, sometimes corresponding with that of the Tenor, sometimes with that of the Bassus. Additional parts for the chansons *a 7* and *a 8* (nos. 21–29) are included in the six partbooks, but in no consistent arrangement. (Their locations are specified in the Critical Notes, below.) Complete sets of the six partbooks are owned by the Österreichische Nationalbibliothek, Vienna, and the Bayerische Staatsbibliothek, Munich. A copy of the Tenor book alone can be found in the Archivo del Musica el Cabildo in Zaragoza, Spain, and copies of the Superius, Contratenor, Tenor, and Bassus books are in the Gemeentemuseum in The Hague.

Unlike the first three books of chansons, Pevernage's last book does not consist exclusively of his own music. One piece in the volume, no. 27, *Un jour l'amant et l'amie*, is a chanson by Orlando di Lasso. The appearance of the name "Orlando" at the bottom of the page in each of the partbooks acknowledges the composer of this chanson, which had appeared originally in the *Mellange d'Orlande de Lassus* (Paris: Le Roy & Ballard, 1570). Why Pevernage included this piece in his *Livre quatrième* is not known. Perhaps he merely wanted to enhance his volume with a piece by that popular composer. More likely he intended it as a tribute to a composer whose work he admired and made use of as a model for some of his own. In any case, the practice of including one piece by a composer other than the one who was chiefly represented in a volume such as this was not uncommon at the time.[7]

With the exception of the two Latin-texted pieces that conclude Book IV, the contents are grouped primarily by voicing. The twenty six-voice chansons that make up the bulk of the volume are followed by two seven-voice chansons, five eight-voice chansons, and two seven-voice motets. The disposition of voices in each of the six-voice chansons is either SSCTBB or SSCTTB (C = Contratenor, or Alto). Most of the chansons *a 7* and *a 8* are for double choir, and their voicing varies as follows:

No. 21	SST - CTTB
No. 22	S(C)TB - STB
Nos. 23–24	SSCT - SCTB
Nos. 25–27	SCTB - SCTB
Nos. 28–29	SSCCTBB

In no. 22 the Contratenor functions with both groups. In assembling the parts into score format in this volume, the editor has followed the divisions designated above, except in no. 26, *Bon jour mon coeur*. In this piece the voice groupings vary, and, although the SCTB-SCTB grouping predominates, the editor has chosen to score the voices from highest to lowest: SSCCTTBB.

As in Pevernage's Books I–III, the chansons are also grouped according to mode, with those of the same mode placed together.[8] Surprisingly, the modal groupings of the seven- and eight-voice chansons fit into this scheme also.

a 6	Nos. 1–3	Dorian on D
	Nos. 4–7	Hypomixolydian on G
	Nos. 8–10	Aeolian on A
	Nos. 11–12	Hypodorian on D
	Nos. 13–15	Hypoionian on C
	Nos. 16–20	Dorian on G
a 7	Nos. 21–22	Dorian on G
a 8	Nos. 23–25	Hypodorian on G
	No. 26	Mixolydian on G

The placement of no. 27, the chanson by Orlando di Lasso, and of nos. 28 and 29, the two motets, at the end of *Livre quatrième* is determined, of course, by their unique character rather than their modes. The distinction between authentic and plagal modes in the above list is made solely according to the ranges and tessituras of the voices. Voices lie approximately a fourth lower in the pieces in the plagal modes than in the authentic modes, but the name of the mode is determined by the Tenor. Although there appears to be no difference in the music itself between pieces in the authentic and plagal forms of the mode, the careful arrangement of Pevernage's volumes shows that musicians were still conscious of the distinction.

Book IV contains both *chansons spirituelles* and *chansons profanes*, although the latter predominate and include several poems (e.g., *La belle Marguerite*, *Le Rossignol plaisant*, and *Bon jour mon coeur*) set by other sixteenth-century musicians also. A number of the texts set in Book IV are the work of leading poets of the sixteenth century, particularly Clément Marot, Philippe Desportes, and Pierre de Ronsard. The presence of their verse gives evidence of Pevernage's generally cultivated taste in poetry. The remaining poet whose work Pevernage set, Jan van der Noot, wrote in both French and Flemish and was one of the leading Belgian poets of his day; it would probably be unfair to judge him by the quality of the functional poem (the *Louange de la ville d'Anvers*) that appears here. Table 1 lists all the known authors of texts set by Pevernage in Book IV and cites the poetic form or genre of the texts.[9]

Table 1

Chanson	Title	Poet	Form or Genre
Nos. 1–3	Clio, chantons disertement	van der Noot	*louange*
Nos. 4–5	Depuis le triste poinct	Desportes	*sonnet*
No. 6	Douce liberté desirée	Desportes	*chanson*
No. 7	Si je vy en peine	Marot	*chanson*
No. 10	Là où scavez sans vous	Marot	*rondeau*
No. 19	Vous perdez temps	Marot	*chanson*
No. 20	O bien-heureux	Desportes	*chanson*
No. 22	Quand je vous aim'	Marot	*epigramme*
Nos. 23–24	Que ferez-vous	Desportes	*dialogue*
No. 26	Bon jour mon coeur	Ronsard	*chanson*

In addition, the anonymous *Oncques amour ne fut* (no. 17) and *Le Rossignol plaisant et gracieux* (no. 21) can be traced to an anthology of verse published in 1543, *La fleur des poésies françoyses*, although they appeared in subsequent anthologies as well.[10]

Several of the pieces in the *Livre quatrième* deserve special attention. *Bon jour mon coeur* (no. 26) has as its text the Ronsard poem known to musicians through di Lasso's setting. Pevernage's eight-voice setting is, in fact, a parody of the four-voice version of di Lasso.[11] All of the material of the model is present in the later setting, and Pevernage has extended his piece to twice the length of the original through repetition and addition of some new material.

Two of the chansons appear to be occasional pieces. One is the setting of Jan van der Noot's *louange* to the city of Antwerp (nos. 1–3) discussed above. The other, *O viateur qui par cy passe* (nos. 13–15), also a chanson of three *parties*, has as its text an epitaph for a Charles of Burgundy. Stellfeld claims that the music was composed in honor of the fifteenth-century Burgundian duke, Charles the Bold (d. 1477); but, although some circumstantial events of the mid-sixteenth century lend credence to the suggestion that Pevernage might have written such a piece nearly a century after Charles's death, the words of the text clearly do not apply to the duke.[12] The Charles of the chanson describes himself as one who has traveled in the service of princes, then retired, and, finally, died unexpectedly while putting his affairs in order. Two possible candidates emerge from the vast stream of progeny from the house of Burgundy. One is Charles de Bourgogne (1490– ?), Lord of Bredam, Fremont, and Fallais; he was the son of Baudouin de Bourgogne (ca. 1436–1508),[13] who, in turn, was a bastard son of Duke Philip the Good. This Charles served as Chamberlain to Charles V and as a member of the emperor's *Conseil d'Etat*, and, although the location and date of this Charles's death are not known, it would not be unlikely that he would be retired from service and pass away sometime during Pevernage's compositional career. However, one would not expect him to be referred to, as he is in the chanson text, as an "ambassador to princes." Perhaps a more likely candidate is his son, also Charles de Bourgogne (d. 1581), Lord of Sommelsdycke, *Ecuyer* of George of Austria, prince-bishop of Liège.[14] While the title *Ecuyer* (Esquire) tells us nothing of his duties for the prince-bishop, it allows for the possibility that Charles traveled on his behalf. Moreover, the date of this Charles's death, 19 December 1581, falls during the prime of Pevernage's career.

The two short motets that conclude the volume are Latin table blessings.[15] Pevernage had concluded Books I and III with motets also—Book I ends with a *Pater noster*, and Book III closes with four motets, the last of which is also a prayer. Other table graces, but in French rather than in Latin, appear among Pevernage's chansons of Book I; they are settings of Marot's popular *Consecration de la table* and *Action de graces*.

On the last page of the *Livre quatrième*, after the

table of contents and across from the text of the *Louange de la ville d'Anvers*, is the poem by Gheesdalius mentioned on p. vii of this Introduction.

In Musicam Andreae Pevernagii.

Musica cui primas tribuet Symphonia partes,
Qui regat Harmonicae plectra sonora Lyrae?
Non hic Thrax Orpheus, non Methymneus Arion,
Non Linus aut Pylades, non Philomelus erit;
Non, qui Terpandrum vicit modulamine, Carneus;
Non, quem dis aluit Socratis arca, Conus;
Auditorve Stagiritae Menedemus; Jopasve
Aeneae citharam qui sonuit profugo;
Non, sibi quem cecinisse ferunt, Aspendius; aut, qui
Miletum celebrat pectine, Timotheus;
Non Phoebi soboles, hac clarus in arte, Philamon
Non qui Thebanae conditor arcis erat;
Non alii veteres Lyrici, Psaltae, Citharoedi,
Quos jactat Latium, Graecia quosve canit.
Namque alios longa exstinxere oblivia, quorum
Vix apud Historicos nomina comperias;
Quosdam vana truces mentitur Fabula tauros
Flexisse, aut rapidas deliniisse tigres.
Nil itaque illorum nostris dat Aphonia seclis,
Quo tetricas mentes exhilarare queant.
Ergo cui tribuet primas Symphonia partes,
Qui regat Harmonicae plectra canora Lyrae?
Hesperia artifices fovet, atque Oenotria magnos:
Orlandi Bavaros mulcet amoena chelys:
Gallia Claudino, Maillardo, Certone guadet;
Phonascosque colit terrae Britanna suos:
Unus at in nostris est Pevernagius oris,
Utile qui dulci miscuit, atque pium.
Cujus Christicolum divina Melodia sensus
Afficit, omnigenis exhilaratque sonis.
Qui superos, hominesque rudes, dirosque leones,
Qui chalybem, silvas, marmora, saxa trahit.
Huic igitur primas tribuat Symphonia partes,
Hic regat Harmonicae plectra canora Lyrae.
Quo duce, dulce melos calami, citharaeque loquuntur:
Quo fine, apud Belgas Musica muta silet.

(For the Music of André Pevernage

To whom will Symphonia give the primacy to ply the sonorous plectrum of the harmonious lyre? This one will not be Thracian Orpheus, nor Methymnean Arion, and it will not be Linus, Pylades, or Philomelus. Neither will it be he who surpasses Terpander with his music, namely, Carneus; nor he whom the treasure of Socrates supported for the gods, namely, Connus; nor Menedemus, the student of the Stagirite [Aristotle]; nor Iopas, who played the lyre for Aeneas the fugitive; nor he whom they say sang to himself, the Aspendian; nor he who makes famous Miletus with his music, namely Timotheus; nor Philamon, the descendant of Phoebus, and famous in this art; nor he who was the founder of the citadel of Thebes; nor the other Lyric poets, psaltery players, or those who sing with the kithera, who are the boast of Greece and Rome. For some of these are buried in long oblivion, and you can scarcely find their names among the writers of history, while lying Fable tells us that others attached fierce bulls to their chariots or tamed ferocious tigers. Thus the silence of history gives none of these to our age to delight gloomy hearts.

Therefore, to whom will Symphonia give the primacy to ply the sonorous plectrum of the harmonious lyre? Italy produces great artists; the charming lyre of Orlando soothes the hearts of the Bavarians. France delights in Claudin, Maillard, and Certon. Britain also produces its choral directors. But at our shores Pevernage is the one who mixes the useful and the pious with the pleasant. His divine melody charms the hearts of Christians and delights them with sounds of every kind. He enchants the gods above, illiterate people, fierce lions, steel, forests, rocks, and seas. And so let Symphonia grant primacy to him; let him ply the sonorities of the harmonious lyre. Under his leadership, the reeds and the strings sing a sweet song; at his death, Music will fall still and silent among the Belgians.)

The impeccable Classical Latin and informed allusions of Gheesdalius's paean make a fine tribute to the chapel master of Antwerp.

Other Chansons: Works from *Le Rossignol musical* and the *Bicinia, sive cantiones*

During the last third of the sixteenth century, publishers favored volumes devoted to works by a single composer. Nevertheless, collections comprised of music by a variety of composers were also still issued. Although all of Pevernage's madrigals appeared in such collections, only a few of his chansons did. All of these chansons have been extracted from their source anthologies and included here, after the chansons of Book IV (see pp. 159–171).

The chanson *a 2*, *Deux que le trait d'Amour*, has as its text a *sonnet* of Philippe Desportes.[16] Pevernage set the poem as a *pièce liée* of three *parties* (nos. [4]–[6]), which was printed in a collection of *bicinia* published by Phalèse and Bellère. The volume's full title describes its contents:

Bicinia, sive cantiones suavissimae duarum vocum, tam divinae musices tyronibus, quam ejusdem artis peritioribus magno usui futurae, nec non et quibusius Instrumentis accommodae: ex praeclaris hujus aetatis Auctoribus collectae: quarum Catalogum pagella sequens explicat (Antwerp: Phalèse and Bellère, 1590)[17]

In addition to the Pevernage chanson, the volume contains motets by di Lasso and Josquin, chansons by Gerard de Turnhout, Jhan Gero, and Corneille and Jean Verdonck; madrigals by Giammateo Asola, Gero, C. Verdonck, and Pevernage (*La vita fugge*); and instrumental pieces by di Lasso, Pomponio Nenna, and others. *Deux que le trait d'Amour* appears on folios 9 and 10 of the *Bicinia, sive cantiones*. The style of this chanson is thoroughly contrapuntal; in fact, the voices imitate each other in inversion throughout.

The remaining three chansons of Pevernage were printed in another collection issued by Phalèse:

Le Rossignol musical des Chansons de diverses et excellens autheurs de nostre temps à quatre, cinc, et six parties. Nouvellement recueillé et mises ises en lumière (Antwerp: Phalèse, 1597)[18]

Among other composers represented in this volume are J. P. Sweelinck, Le Jeune, de Monte, George de la Hele, Eustache du Caurroy, and Philippe Rogier. The three chansons of Pevernage, all for four voices, appear on folios 2, 8, and 9 of the partbooks. *Si dessus voz levres de roses* (no. [1]) has as its text an epigram by Philippe Desportes that appeared originally in the poet's *Diverses amours*.[19] *Ma mignonne debonnaire* (no. [2]) seems to be not an independent chanson but the second *partie* of a *pièce liée*. This is suggested by both the text and the music. The text comes from Marot's Chanson XXX, where it constitutes the second strophe.[20] Although it would have been unusual, it is not inconceivable that Pevernage set only the second strophe of a poem. However, there is strong musical evidence suggesting that this chanson is part of a *pièce liée*. All of Pevernage's chansons that stand alone begin and end in the same mode, and the pitches on which voices enter in opening points of imitation in these pieces are the final and either the fifth or fourth degree, depending on the mode. On the other hand, in his *pièces liées* the first piece of a pair of chansons usually terminates with a half-cadence (or on the final of a secondary mode), and the second piece begins with the same harmony—that is, with the dominant or subdominant chord or imitative entrances on its final and fourth or fifth degree—and quickly returns to the primary mode. That *Ma mignonne debonnaire*, which is firmly in Dorian on G, begins with entrances on A, D, and then G suggests that it was originally paired with a setting of the first strophe, also in Dorian on G, but concluding with a D-chord. However, no setting by Pevernage of the first strophe is known to be extant. The third Pevernage chanson in *Le Rossignol musical*, *Pour estr' aymé par grande loyauté* (no. [3]), has as its text an anonymous five-line *rondeau*.

Since *Le Rossignol musical* was published six years after the composer's death, one wonders where the publisher obtained these Pevernage chansons. Were they commissioned from the composer before his death and held until 1597, were they obtained from Pevernage's widow, or were they circulating in manuscript until they were published in *Le Rossignol*? The inclusion of an incomplete *pièce liée* would lead us to suspect that these chansons were not submitted by the composer, at least not as we find them here.

Editorial Commentary

This edition of *Livre quatrième des chansons . . .* (1591) is based on the complete set of six partbooks in the Bayerische Staatsbibliothek, Munich (shelf number Mus pr 32/3), which was made available to the editor on microfilm. The sixteenth-century original is clearly printed and easily read. The microfilm copies of *Bicinia, sive cantiones* and *Le Rossignol musical* used for this edition were, respectively, those of the Universitetsbiblioteket of Uppsala and the Biblioteka Polskiej Akademii Nauk of Gdansk. All editorial additions and alterations except titles are enclosed in brackets in this volume. The only titles that appear in the sources are those of the two motets, and these have been retained here. All others are added by the editor and simply reproduce all or part of the first line of text. The barlines drawn through the staves are also editorial. Solid horizontal brackets (┌──┐) mark notes that appear as ligatures in the source. Broken horizontal brackets (┌ ┐) mark coloration, which appears only in no. 9, as "eye-music" for the phrase "Chasse ces tenebres."

Because of the simple syllabic texture used by Pevernage and the great care taken at both the Plantin and Phalèse & Bellère firms for accuracy of text placement, no problems of text underlay were encountered. In the sources, all repetitions of text are either written out or indicated with the sign *ij*. No additional editorial repetitions were necessary.

For the most part, spelling and punctuation of the texts remain unaltered. However, all abbreviations, including ampersands, have been written out, and archaic spellings with "u," "v," and "i" have been changed to their modern forms whenever the original version might confuse the reader, as, for instance, in *ie viue* (*je vive*). The use of contractions and apostrophes to indicate elisions follows the source. Accents have been added to vowels where they were omitted from the source (either by mistake or because the practice was not standard) and where their absence might affect pronunciation or confuse the reader. Spellings have otherwise not been modernized, even though pronunciation should not differ substantially from modern forms of the same words. The most frequently encountered archaism is the obsolete "s," which would not have been pronounced.[21] In this edition, syllable divisions in the French texts indicate whether the "s" is to be pronounced or not: where the "s" falls before the division, it is silent; where it falls after the division, it must be pronounced. For example, in *mais-tre* and *vos-tre* the "s" is silent; in *tri-stesse* and *e-sprits* the "s" is pronounced. Another common archaism is seen in spellings with "oi," where modern French has "ai," as in *regnoit* (*regnait*), *resistoit* (*resistait*), or *apparoistre* (*apparaître*). Again, the modern "ai" sound should be used.

Punctuation follows the source for the most part, but frequent editorial changes were made for the sake of clarity. In many cases, the punctuation following a phrase of text in the source is not clear because the final appearance of the phrase is indicated with the *ij* sign, and thus includes no punctuation. Full stops (usually indicated in the edition with a colon) were added where the comma used in the source seemed insufficient, or where a colon was lacking in the source because the phrase of text makes its last appearance by means of a repeat sign.

The editorial incipit of the music gives the clef, key signature, mensuration sign, first note, and name of each part as found in the sources. For the G- and moveable C- and F-clefs of the sources, this edition uses the treble, tenor G-clef, and bass clef. In the six-voice pieces, the Sexta always functions as an additional superius part. The placement of the Quinta voice varies from piece to piece, depending on its range, although its name has been retained. Where its range corresponds with that of the Superius, the Quinta is placed on the fourth staff up. Where the range of the Quinta is like that of the Tenor, it appears on the middle staff. Ranges of all voices are indicated immediately before the modern clef. (Performers should note that the range does not always give a reliable impression of the tessitura; for instance, on occasion the bottom note of the specified range may appear only once or twice in certain works, and the most common low note in the piece may otherwise be a fourth above that indicated in the range-finder.) Note values in this edition have been reduced by half, except for the final note of each piece, which is a longa in the source and has been transcribed here as a whole-note with a fermata.

Pevernage used two mensuration signs, C and ¢, but with no apparent distinction in musical styles or rhythmic values. It is likely that Pevernage, like many of his contemporaries, did not intend different meanings for the two signs, but they have nevertheless been retained.

Accidentals that appear within the staff are original; those that appear above the staff are editorial and include both cautionary accidentals and *musica ficta*. Editorial accidentals have been supplied sparingly, and consideration has been given to general sixteenth-century practices as well as to Pevernage's own idiosyncracies. Where sharp signs in the sources cancel flats, they have been changed to naturals in the edition. In the sources, an accidental is valid only for successive notes of the same pitch, unless the second statement of that pitch begins a new phrase, in which case the validity of the accidental is not always clear. In the sources, an accidental is canceled either by a rest or by an intervening note of a different pitch, and this system is also followed here, since it seems clearest in music with such frequent and temporary pitch alterations—and thus accidentals that are redundant in modern practice are preserved here. Both original and editorial accidentals should be considered valid for consecutive notes within measures. In a given voice, where previously inflected pitches recur after intervening notes and the accidental must be invalidated, an editorial reminder is provided above the staff.

The shape of the melodic lines in many places may tempt the reader to raise or lower pitches in accordance with the rules of *musica ficta*. However, performers must be careful to take note of the other voices: such alterations will often result in cross-relations within a chord or in augmented harmonies. The extreme care, frequency, and consistency with which Pevernage supplied accidentals in all his chansons make it doubtful that he intended the performer to add many of his own. A notable departure from normal sixteenth-century practice in this respect is his avoidance of diminished harmonies in the first inversion for penultimate chords at cadences (i.e., dim. VII^6–I). Although he invariably supplied a sharp to the third where the penultimate chord lies a fourth below the cadence chord (and where anyone familiar with the style would add one anyway), he consistently left unaltered those penultimate chords that have their roots a major second below the cadence chord. Pevernage's consistency in this matter suggests that he intended the VII^6 to remain unaltered.

Critical Notes

The following list cites errors in the sources and other discrepancies between the present edition and the *Livre quatrième des chansons . . .* (1591), the *Bicinia, sive cantiones*, and *Le Rossignol musical*. Pitches are designated according to the usual system, wherein middle C is c', the C above middle C is c'', and so forth.

Livre quatrième des chansons . . . (1591)

No. 19—Mm. 31ff., original text reads "Cessez vous . . ."; correction here ("Cessez *voz* grand' audace") conforms with the Mayer edition of Marot's poem. See *Oeuvres lyriques*, ed. C. A. Mayer (London, 1964), p. 202.

No. 21—Source designations for the two choruses read: *"Primi chori"* and *"Secundi chori." Primi chori:* S I is in Superius partbook; S II is in Sexta partbook; T is in Sexta partbook. *Secondi chori*: C is in Contratenor partbook; T [I] is in Tenor partbook; T [II] is in Quinta partbook; B is in Bassus partbook.

No. 22—Source designations for the two choruses read: *"Primi chori"* and *"Secundi chori." Primi chori:* S is in Superius partbook; C is in Contratenor partbook; T is in Tenor partbook; B is in Bassus partbook. *Secondi chori*: S is in Sexta partbook; T is in Sexta partbook; B is in Quinta partbook. M. 29, Tenor, *Primi chori*, note 4 has a cautionary sharp in the source.

Nos. 23–24—Source designations for the two choruses read: *"Primi chori"* and *"Secundi chori." Primi chori:* S I is in Superius partbook; S II is in Contratenor partbook; C is in Contratenor partbook; T is in Tenor partbook. *Secondi chori*: S is in Sexta partbook; C is in Sexta partbook; T is in Quinta partbook; B is in Bassus partbook.

Nos. 25–26—S I is in Superius partbook; C I is in Contratenor partbook; T I is in Tenor partbook; B I is in Bassus partbook; S II and C II are in Sexta partbook; T II and B II are in Quinta partbook.

No. 27—S I and C I are in Sexta partbook; T I is in Tenor partbook; B I is in Quinta partbook; S II is in Superius partbook; C II is in Contratenor partbook; T II and B II are in Bassus partbook. Mm. 15–17, all parts, text has "jouet" in source. Mm. 28–29, all parts, original text has "Le desous" in source.

Nos. 28 and 29—S [I] is in Superius partbook; S II is in Sexta partbook; C [I] is in Contratenor partbook; C II is in Sexta partbook; T is in Tenor partbook; Quinta is in Sexta partbook; B is in Bassus partbook. Note: The Quinta appears on the last page of the Sexta partbook. Since S II and C II are printed on the previous folio spread, this would not be easily accessible.

Other Chansons

Nos. [4]–[6]—Several corrections have been made in the text. These were based on the poem as it appears in Desportes, *Diverses amours et autres oeuvres mellées*, ed. Victor E. Graham (Geneva, 1963), p. 29.

No. [6]—M. 1, both parts, text reads "C'est" in the source rather than "Cest." M. 8, both parts, text reads "no" in source rather than "nous." Mm. 22 ff., both parts, text reads "seule" in the source rather than "sale."

Notes

1. The French term *parties* is used here to refer to the constituent pieces of *pièces liées* (chansons consisting of two or more separate pieces). Since *pièces liées* are, in a sense, single multipartite units, their numbers will be joined with an N-dash (e.g., nos 1–3).

2. See also, Gerald R. Hoekstra, "The Chansons of André Pevernage (1542/43–1591)" (The Ohio State University, Ph.D. diss., 1975).

3. Jean Moretus (d. 1600) married Plantin's second daughter, Martine. Along with another associate named Raphaelengius, he ran the Antwerp firm during Plantin's absence, from 1583 to 1585. When Plantin died in July 1589, he left the Antwerp establishment to Moretus and the Leiden branch of the firm to Raphaelengius. See J.-A. Stellfeld, *Bibliographie des éditions musicales Plantiniènnes* (Brussels: Publications de l'Académie royale de Belgique, 1949), pp. 9–10.

4. According to J.-A. Stellfeld, *Andries Pevernage: zijn leven—zijne werken* (Louvain: De vlaamsche Drukkerij, N.V., 1943), p. 60, the *Louange* appeared also in van der Noot's *Poetische Werken* of 1592 (Antwerp: Arnoud 's Coninckx).

5. "Andries Pevernage sangmeester van Onser Vrouwen Kerk alhier 50 lb voor eene vereeringe ende recompensie van dat hy ter eeren deser Stadt gemaeckt heeft zekeren muzyckboeck met ses, seven ende acht partyen waeraff hy oock der vs. Stadt een exemplaar ryckelyck ge-

bonden geschoncken heeft." Stadrekening, 1591. Acte Coll. 1 Februari, 1591. Quoted by Stellfeld, *Andries Pevernage*, p. 64.

6. Ibid.

7. As examples I cite the following: Severin Cornet in his *Chansons françoyses* (1581), also published by Plantin, included one piece by Corneille Verdonck; and Sweelinck included four Verdonck pieces in his chanson volume of 1594, published by Phalèse.

8. See the Introductions to the editions of Pevernage's Books I, II, and III (RRRen vols. LX–LXII) for citations of similar groupings according to modes.

9. Modern editions of most of these poems are available in the following: Philippe Desportes, *Les amours d'Hippolyte*, ed. Victor E. Graham (Geneva: Libraire Droz, 1960) and *Diverses amours et autres oeuvres mellées*, ed. Victor E. Graham (Geneva: Libraire Droz, 1963); Clément Marot, *Oeuvres lyriques*, ed. C. A. Mayer (London: University of London, Athlone Press, 1964) and *Les epigrammes*, ed. C. A. Mayer (London: University of London, Athlone Press, 1970); and Pierre de Ronsard, *Les oeuvres de Pierre de Ronsard: texte de 1587*, ed. Isadore Silver (Chicago: The University of Chicago Press, 1966).

10. Cf. Frédéric Lachèvre, *Bibliographie des récueils collectifs de poésies du XVIe siècle* (Paris: Edouard Champion, 1922). Both poems reappeared in *La Fleur de Dame* (1548) and *Le courtizan amoureux* (Lyon, 1583). Although the latter collection is not included in Lachèvre's bibliography, the title is furnished by Stellfeld (*Andries Pevernage*, p. 68) as the source of *Le Rossignol plaisant*.

11. See Gerald R. Hoekstra, "An 8-Voice Parody of Lassus: Pevernage's *Bon jour mon coeur*," *Early Music* VII (July 1979): 367–77. Lassus's chanson appeared initially in the *Sesieme livre des chansons par Orlande de Lassus* (Paris, 1565). It appeared subsequently in four other collections, and each of these, as well as the original volume, was reissued a number of times. Modern editions of the chanson appear in the *Historical Anthology of Music* (Cambridge, Mass.: Harvard University Press, 1946), I: 159, and in the Lassus *Werke*, ed. F. X. Haberl and Adolf Sandberger (Leipzig: Breitkopf & Härtel, 1894–1926), XII: 100.

12. See Stellfeld, *Andries Pevernage*, p. 61. Stellfeld cites in support of his claim the following. Holy Roman Emperor Charles V, a descendant of Charles the Bold, obtained permission near the end of his reign to transport the body of his illustrious ancestor to the church of Notre Dame in Bruges. This took place with great ceremony in 1550. After the emperor's death in 1558, his son and successor, Philip II, ordered that a lavish tomb be erected for the body of Duke Charles and, in 1563, instituted an annual service in his memory (see also Th. Juste, "Charles surnommé Le Téméraire," *Biographie nationale de Belgique* [Brussels: H. Thiry, 1872], II: 522–23). This was the same year that André Pevernage served as chapel master of the church of St. Salvator in Bruges. However, it should be noted that a chanson is hardly appropriate for an occasion of such solemnity, which probably would have required a motet. Furthermore, Charles the Bold died on the battlefield at Nancy and can hardly be said to have been putting his affairs in order upon retirement.

13. Marcel Berge, "Les bâtards de la Maison de Bourgogne et leur descendence," *L'Intermediaire des généalogistes* (Nov. 1955), p. 381. I am grateful to Professor Richard Vaughan of the University of Hull for bringing this article to my attention. Baudouin de Bourgogne, Lord of Fallais, Peer Lovinghem, Manilly, Bredam and Sommelsdycke, was one of twenty-six illegitimate children of Philip the Good. He, in turn, fathered six legitimate children, of whom one was Charles, and four bastards. The date of Charles's death is not known.

14. Ibid., p. 388. Berge tells us that this Charles was arrested as a participant in the Reformed cause in 1549 but released the following year; the Lordship of Fallais was restored to him in 1559. Seven of the elder Charles's nine children are known to have been Reformed converts or to have been associated in some way with the Reformed cause (see p. 387).

15. Carleton Sprague Smith, "Table Blessings Set to Music" in *The Commonwealth of Music*, ed. Gustave Reese and Rose Brandel (New York: The Free Press, 1965). Smith does not mention in his article the three Latin table blessings of Pevernage (Bk. III, no. 25, and Bk. IV, nos. 28 and 29).

16. Desportes, *Diverses amours*, p. 29.

17. Copies of *Bicinia, sive cantiones* are held by the Staats- und Stadt- bibliothek, Augsburg, and the Universitetsbiblioteket, Uppsala. A copy in the Bibliothèque du Conservatoire, Paris, is lacking some pages in the Superius partbook.

18. The only complete copy of *Le Rossignol musical* is the one in the Biblioteka Polskiej Akademii Nauk, Gdansk. A copy of the Tenor partbook, is held by the Universitetsbiblioteket, Uppsala. A set of the edition of 1598 lacking only the Quinta partbook is found in the Bibliothèque royale de Belgique, Brussels; a copy of the Quinta may be found in the collection of Westminster Abbey, London.

19. Desportes, *Diverses amours*, p. 200.

20. Marot, *Oeuvres lyriques*, p. 198. The first strophe of this poem begins: "J'ayme le cueur de m'Amye."

21. Those who desire a guide to pronunciation are referred to Jeannine Alton and Brian Jeffery, *Bele Buche e Bele Parleure: A Guide to the Pronunciation of Medieval and Renaissance French for Singers and Others* (London: Tecla Editions, 1976).

Texts and Translations

The following translations were made by the editor with the helpful advice and guidance of Dr. William Huseman. They are literal rather than poetic translations.

Livre quatrième des chansons . . . (1591)

No. 1 [*1. partie*] Jan van der Noot

Clio, chantons disertement la gloire
Et le beau los de la ville d'Anvers,
Faisons son los au temple de memoire,
Vivr' à jamais par l'ardeur de mes vers.

(Clio, let us sing eloquently the glory
And praises of the city of Antwerp,
Let us make its praises live forever
In the temple of memory by the ardor of my verse.)

No. 2 *2. partie*

Du peupl' aussi et de la Republique,
Chantons l'honneur, et du noble Senat,
Tant moderé, tant sag' et magnifique,
Qu'il faict beau veoir si prudent Magistrat.

(Of the people also and of the Republic
Let us sing the honors, and of the noble Senate,
So moderate, so wise and magnificent,
That it is beautiful to see such a prudent Magistrate.)

No. 3 *3. partie*

Chantons aussi l'honneur des belles dames,
Tant richement ornées de douceur,
Et de beautez tant des corps que des ames,
Qu'on ne leur peut donner assez d'honneur.

(Let us sing also the honors of the beautiful women,
So richly adorned with gentility,
And having such beauty of body and soul
That one cannot honor them enough.)

No. 4 [*1. partie*] Philippe Desportes

Depuis le triste poinct de ma fraisle naissance,
Et que dans le berceau pleurant je feu posé,
Quel jour marqué de blanc m'a tant favorisé,
Que de l'ombre d'un bien j'ay eu la jouissance?
A pein' estoient seiché les pleurs de mon enfance,
Qu'au froid, au chaud, à l'eau, je me vey exposé
D'amour, de la fortune, et des grands maistrisé,
Qui m'ont payé de vent pour toute recompense.

(Since the sad moment of my weak birth,
And since I was laid crying in the cradle,
Which day under the sun has so favored me
That I have had the pleasure of even a shadow of some good?
The tears of my infancy were hardly dried,
When I was exposed to cold, to heat, and to water
By love, by fortune, and by the powerful,
Who paid me nothing but wind as recompense.)

No. 5 *2. partie*

J'en suis fable du monde, et mes vers dispersez
Sont les signes piteux des maux que j'ay passez,
Quand tant de fiers tyrans ravageoyent mon courage:
Toy qui m'ostes le joug, et me fais respirer,
O Seigneur, pour jamais vueilles moy retirer
De la terre d'Egypte, et d'un si dur servage.

(I am the talk of the world for it, and my dispersed verses
Are the piteous signs of ills that I endured
When so many proud tyrants ravaged my courage.
You who remove from me the yoke and give me breath,
O Lord, deign to take me away forever from
Out of the land of Egypt and from such harsh bondage.)

No. 6 Philippe Desportes

Douce liberté desirée,
Deesse, où t'es tu retirée,
Me laissant en captivité?
Helas! de moy ne te destourne,
Retourn' o liberté, retourne,
Retourn' o douce liberté.

(Sweet, longed-for liberty,
Goddess, where do you hide yourself,

Leaving me in captivity?
Alas! Do not turn away from me.
Return, o liberty, return,
Return, o sweet liberty.)

No. 7 Clément Marot

Si je vy en pein' et en langueur,
De bon gré je le porte,
Puis que celle qui a mon coeur,
Languist de mesme sorte.

(If I live in pain and in languor,
Willingly I endure it,
Since she who has my heart
Languishes in the same way.)

No. 8 [*1. partie*]

La nuict le jour je ne fay que songer:
Tout m'est contraire, et ne puis resister:
Le coeur me fault, mes esprits sommeillant
Sont agitez comm' un ruisseau coulant.

(Night and day all I do is dream:
All is against me, and I cannot resist;
My heart fails me, my drooping spirits
Are agitated like a rushing stream.)

No. 9 *2. partie*

Haste le pas et destruy ces douleurs;
Chasse ces tenebres, ces travaux et langueurs,
Ou bien la mort, par la fier' Atropos,
Soit avancé, si avray-je repos.

(Hasten your steps and destroy these sorrows,
Chase away these shadows, these labors and languors,
Or else let death by the proud Atropos
Come; then will I have rest.)

No. 10 Clément Marot

Là où sçavez sans vous ne puis venir,
Vous estes cil qui pouvez subvenir
Facilement à mon cas et affaire,
Et des heureux de ce monde me faire,
Sans qu' aucun mal vous en puiss' advenir.

(There, where you know that without you I cannot come,
You are the one who can help relieve
Easily in my predicament
And make me one of the happy men in this world,
Without bringing any harm to yourself.)

No. 11

La belle Marguerite,
C'est une noble fleur,
Combien qu' ell' est petite,
Ell' est de grand' valeur.

(The beautiful Daisy
Is a noble flower;
Although it is small,
It is of great worth.)

No. 12

Le plus grand contentement
Que peut en amour avoir
L'homme de bon jugement,
C'est de s'esjouir à voir
Celle qui par bon devoir
Scait vertu à beauté joindre,
Faisant à chacun sçavoir,
Que nul ne la peut disjoindre.

(The greatest contentment
That a man of good judgment
Can have in love
Is to have the pleasure of seeing
Her who for duty's sake
Knows how to join virtue to beauty,
Making known to all
That nothing can lure her away.)

No. 13 [*1. partie*]

O viateur qui par cy passe,
Arreste toy, ne vois tu pas ce,
Que te requiert, desja passé,
Dir' au defunct, *Sis in pace*.

(O traveler who passes by,
Stop; do you not see this
That requires you, already past,
To say to the dead, *Rest in Peace*?)

No. 14 *2. partie*

Ayant couru en diverses provinces,
Par mer, par terre, en post' et autrement,
En furnissant ambassades des Princes,
Y consumant du mien abondamment.

(Having traversed different provinces
By sea, by land, by coach and otherwise,
Serving as ambassador for princes,
Consuming thus of my own abundantly.)

No. 15 *3. partie*

Retourné suis en ma maison, Comment?
Recompensé d'un bel Adieu de court,
Dont de regret qu'on me tranchoit du sourd,
Tout retiré redressant ma besoingne,
Mort m'a surpris, qui, pour le faire court,
A cy dessous mis Charles de Bourgoingne.

(I have returned to my home. How?
Repaid by a fine farewell at court,
From which I regret I was cut off by deafness;
Completely retired, trying to straighten out my affairs,
Death surprised me, and—to make it short—
Has buried here Charles of Burgundy.)

No. 16

Je porte tes couleurs, ma dam' et ma maistresse,
Et si veux demourer tousjours ton serviteur,
Ne refuse doncq point mon miserable coeur,
Nul autre fors que toy luy peut donner liesse:
Et comm' en tes couleurs que port' en allegresse,
Du gris l'on voit qui faict le travail ou labeur,
Et du blanc qu'est la foy, et la jaulne couleur,
Laquell' à la bonheur contentement m'addresse,
Ainsi par mon travail, ma foy, et mon espoir,
Meriteray un jour ta bonne grac' avoir,
Ou la fier' Atropos mettra fin à ma vie:
Tousjours j'ay bon espoir, car n'usant de rigueur,
Tu m'as voulu nommer ton petit serviteur,
Et je te nomm' aussi ma maistress' et amie.

(I wear your colors, my lady and my mistress,
And so would always remain your servant;
Do not refuse my miserable heart anything.
None but you can give it happiness.
And just as in your colors, which I wear gladly,
One sees gray, the color of work and labor,
White, which is for faith, and yellow,
Which symbolizes for me happy contentment,
So by my work, my faith, and my hope
Will I one day earn your good grace and favor,
Or the proud Atropos will put an end to my life.
Always I hope, for dealing with me harshly,
You have decided to call me your lowly servant,
And I in turn call you my mistress and lover.)

No. 17

Oncques amour ne fut sans grand' langueur,
Langueur ne fut jamais sans esperance,
Voilà le point, où gist tout le malheur,
Qu'on voit souvent espoir sans jouissance.

(Never was there love without great languor;
Never was there languor without hope;
That is the point where misfortune lies,
That one sees hope without fulfillment.)

No. 18

Vivre ne puis sur terre,
Car mort suis à demy,
Plusieurs me font la guerre,
Et me font ennemy:
O mort, venez moy querre
Sans moy faire mercy.

(I cannot live on earth,
For I am half dead.
Many make war against me
And make me their enemy.
O death, come seek me
Without showing me mercy.)

No. 19 — Clément Marot

Vous perdez temps de me dire mal d'elle,
Gens qui voulez divertir mon entente:
Plus la blamez, plus je la trouve belle;
S'esbahit-on si tant je m'en contente?
La fleur de sa jeunesse,
A vostr' advis rien n'est ce?
N'est ce rien de sa grace?
Cessez voz grand' audace,
Car mon amour vaincra vostre mesdire.
Tel en mesdict, qui pour soy la desire.

(You waste time speaking ill to me of her,
You who would make me change my opinion:
The more you criticize her, the more I find her beautiful;
Does it dumbfound you that I am so content with her?
The flower of her youth—
Does that mean nothing to you?
Is her grace nothing to you?
Put an end to your audacity,
For my love will overcome your vilification.
Only one who desires her for himself would speak so ill of her.)

No. 20 — Philippe Desportes

O bien-heureux qui peut passer sa vie
Entre les siens, franc de hain' et envie,
Parmi les champs, les forests et les bois,
Loing du tumult' et du bruit populaire:
Et qui ne vend sa liberté pour plaire
Aux volontez des Princes et des Rois!

(O, fortunate is he who can pass his life
Among his own, free of hatred and envy,
In the fields, forests, and woods,
Far from the tumult and noise of the crowd,
And who does not sell his freedom in order to satisfy
The wishes of princes and kings!)

No. 21

Le Rossignol plaisant et gracieux,
Habiter veut tousjours au verd bocage,
Aux champs voler, et par tout autres lieux,
Sa liberté aimant mieux que sa cage:
Mais le mien coeur, qui demeur' en ostage
Sous triste dueil qui le tient en ses lacs,
Du Rossignol ne cerche l'avantage,
Ne de son chant recevoir le soulas.

(The nightingale, pleasing and graceful,
Wishes to live always among the green leaves,
To fly to the fields and everywhere else,
Loving its freedom more than its cage.
But this heart of mine, which lives as hostage
To the sadness that holds it in its snares,
Does not look to the nightingale for help,
Nor from its song receive comfort.)

No. 22 — Clément Marot

Quand je vous aim' ardentement,
Vostre beauté tout' autr' efface:
Quand je vous aime froidement,
Vostre beauté fond comme glace.

(When I love you ardently,
Your beauty eliminates all others;
When I love you coldly,
Your beauty melts like ice.)

No. 23 [*1. partie*] — Philippe Desportes

Que ferez-vous, dites ma dame,
Perdant un si fidell' amant?
—Ce que peut fair' un corps sans ame,
Sans yeux, sans pouls, sans mouvement.
—N'en aurez vous plus souvenance
Apres ce rigoreux depart?
—Au coeur qui oubli' en absence
L'amour n'a jamais eu de part.
—De tant d'ennuis qui vous font guerre,
Lequel vous donne plus de peur?
—La crainte qu'en changeant de terre,
Il puiss' aussi changer de coeur.
—N'usez jamais de ce langage,
A sa foy vous faictes grand tort.
—C'est un evident temoignage
Pour monstrer, que j'aime bien fort.
—Son amour si ferm' et si saincte
Doit tenir vostr' esprit contant.
—Je ne puis que je n'aye crainte
De perdre ce que j'aime tant.

(What will you do, tell me, my lady,
Losing such a faithful lover?
—I will do what a body does without a soul,
Without eyes, without pulse, without movement.
—But won't you still have memories
After this cruel departure?
—To the heart that forgets in absence
Love was never really genuine.
—Of all the troubles against which you struggle,
Which one makes you most afraid?
—The fear that in changing countries
He might also have a change of heart.
—Don't ever use such words;
You are doing a great wrong to his faithfulness.
—It is a clear testimony
To show how strongly I love.
—His love so firm and holy
Must keep your spirit contented.
—I cannot help being afraid
Of losing that which I love so much.)

No. 24 *2. partie*

—Auriez-vous beaucoup de tristesse,
S'il venoit à changer de foy?
—Tout autant que j'ay de liesse
Sçachant bien qu'il n'aime que moy.
—Quel est le mal qui vous offense,
Attendant ce departement?
—Tel que d'un qui a eu sentence
Et attend la mort seulement.
—Quoy? vous pensez doncques à l'heure
Qu'il s'en ira mourir d'ennuy?
—Il ne se peut que je ne meure,
Mon esprit s'en va quant à luy.
—Si tel accident vous arrive,
Vostr' amour ne durera pas.
—La vray amour est tousjours vive,
Et ne meurt point par le trespas.

(Would you be greatly saddened
If he were to have a change of heart?
—As much as I have great joy
In knowing well that he loves only me.
—What is the sorrow that disturbs you
While waiting for this departure?
—Like that of one who has been sentenced
And waits only for death.
—What? You think then that when he will go away
You will die of grief?

—It is impossible for me not to die,
My spirit goes away with him.
—If such a thing happens to you
Your love will not last.
—True love lives always
And does not die in the least with death.)

No. 25

Soyons plaisans
tous gallans
en delaissant melancolie,
Buvons d'autant
en menant
tousjours vie gay' et jolie.
Laissans ennuy, prenons nostre plaisir,
Car en la fin le meilleur nous demeure,
Puis qu'il nous faut partir,
Soyons plaisans encore demy heure.

(Let us be happy,
all gallants,
in abandoning melancholy.
Drink to having
and leading always
a life gay and jolly.
Let us leave boredom, let us take our pleasure,
For in the end, the best part remains with us;
Since we must part,
Let us make merry yet for half an hour.)

No. 26 Pierre de Ronsard

Bon jour mon coeur, bon jour ma douce vie,
Bon jour mon oeil, bon jour ma douc' amie:
Hé bon jour ma toute belle,
Ma mignardise, bon jour
Mes delices, mon amour.
Mon doux printemps, ma douce fleur nouvelle,
Mon doux plaisir, ma douce colombelle,
Mon passereau, ma gente tourterelle,
Bon jour ma douce rebelle.

(Good day, my heart, good day, my sweet life,
Good day, my eye, good day, my sweet friend:
Ah, good day, you pretty one,
My darling, good day,
My delight, my love.
My sweet springtime, my sweet young flower,
My sweet pleasure, my sweet dove,
My sparrow, my gentle turtledove,
Good day, my sweet rebel.)

No. 27

Un jour l'amant et l'amie
Sous un buisson j'ay trouvé,
Qui jouoient à l'endormie,
Au beau jeu tant esprouvé,
A couvert
Sur le verd,
L'amant jouait par nature,
Et l'amie
Sa partie
Tenoit tresbonne mesure.

Sous la verde couverture
Le Rossignol j'escoutois,
Qui chantoit à l'aventure
Là dessus à haute voix.
Le Pinson
En chanson
Par devoir faisoit homage,
La Linotte
Sur la motte
Aux amans disoit courage.

(One day I found under a bush
A lover and his lass,
Who were pretending to be asleep;
At the fine game so often undertaken,
Covered
With the green,
The lover was playing his part naturally;
And the lass
Carried her part
In good measure.

Under the green covering
I listened to the nightingale
Who sang freely
Up above with high-pitched voice.
The finch
In song
Through duty paid homage;
The linnet
On the ground
Said to the lovers: courage.)

No. 28

Consecratio mensae

Benedicite, Dominus,
Nos, et ea quae sumus sumpturi, benedicat dextera Christi.
In nomine Patris, et Filii, et Spiritus sancti. Amen.

(Table Blessing)

(Let us praise the Lord with our whole being, even as those at Christ's right hand. In the name of the Father, the Son, and the Holy Spirit. Amen.)

No. 29

Gratiarum actio

Qui nos creavit, redemit, et pavit, sit benedictus in saecula. Amen.

(Grace)

(He who has created, redeemed, and chastizes us,
He must be praised in the world. Amen.)

Other Chansons

No. [1] Philippe Desportes

Si dessus voz levres de roses
Je voy mes liesses decloses,
Mon esprit, ma vie, et mon bien,
Vous ne povez me les defendre:
Par tout le mien je puis reprendre,
Il faut que chacun ait le sien.

(If on your rosy lips
I see my happiness revealed,
My spirit, my life, and my well-being,
You cannot forbid me them.
Everywhere I take what is mine,
Everyone must have his own.)

No. [2] Clément Marot

Ma mignonne debonnaire,
Ceux qui font tant de clameurs
Ne tachent qu'à eux complaire,
Plus qu'à leurs belles amours.
Laissons les en leur folie,
Et en leur melancolie;
Leur amitie cessera,
Sans fin la nostre sera.

(My debonair darling,
Those who make so much clamor
Try only to please themselves
More than their beautiful loves.
Let us leave them in their folly
And in their melancholy;
Their friendship will cease,
Ours will never end.)

No. [3]

Pour estr' aymé par grande loyauté,
Ne regardez à la grande beauté,
Car bien souvent tant plus la dame est belle,
Tant plus elle est à son amy rebelle,
Ne luy montrant que toute cruauté.

(To be loved with great loyalty,
Look not for great beauty,
For often the more beautiful a lady is,
The more rebellious she is to her lover,
Showing only to him every cruelty.)

No. [4] [*1. partie*] Philippe Desportes

Deux que le trait d'Amour touche bien vivement,
N'ont rien qu'un seul penser, qu'un desir, qu'une flame:
Ce n'est dedans deux corps qu'un esprit et une ame,
Et leur souverain bien gist en eux seulement.

(Two that the arrow of Love strikes acutely
Have just one desire and one thought and one passion;
That is to have within two bodies only one spirit and soul
And their supreme well-being rests in them alone.)

No. [5] *2. partie*

Ilz ont en mesme temps égal contentement,
Mesme ennuy d'un seul coup leurs poitrines entame,
Bref leur vie et leur mort pend d'une seule trame
Et comm' un simple corps ilz n'ont qu'un mouvement.

(They have at the same time equal contentment,
The same weariness has cut their breasts with a single blow;
In short, their life and their death hang from a single thread,
And as a single body, they have only one movement.)

No. [6] *3. partie*

Cest amour qui si rare en la terre se treuve
Ne fait qu'un de nos coeurs: les effets en sont preuve;
Nous n'avons qu'un vouloir qu'un' ardeur, qu'un desir.
Que nous peut honorer d'assez digne louange?
L'esprit qui se devise et qui se plaist au change
N'est point touché d'amour, mais d'un sale plaisir.

(This love, which is formed so rarely on earth,
Makes but one of our hearts; the effects are the proof;
We have only one will, one passion, one desire.
What could we honor with enough praise?
The spirit that talks to itself and that is pleased with change
Is not struck by love at all, but only by unclean pleasure.)

LIVRE QVATRIEME

DES CHANSONS

D'ANDRE' PEVERNAGE,

MAISTRE DE LA CHAPELLE

DE L'EGLISE CATHEDRALE

D'ANVERS.

A six, sept, & huict parties.

SVPERIVS.

A ANVERS,

EN L'IMPRIMERIE PLANTINIENNE,

Chez la Vefue, & Iean Mourentorf.

M. D. XCI.

Plate I. André Pevernage: *Livre quatrième des chansons* . . . (1591)
Superius partbook, title page.
(Bayerische Staatsbibliothek, Munich)

AVX NOBLES, PRVDENTS, ET VERTVEVX SEIGNEVRS EDVARD VANDER DILFT, CHARLES MALINEVS BOVRGMAISTRES:

Et aultres Senateurs de la tresfameuse ville d'Anuers.

MESSEIGNEVRS, *Ayant pieça experimenté les bonnes affections, beneuolences, & faueurs de vos S^ries^ tant en particulier qu'en general: apres auoir mis en lumiere l'an passé trois Liures de Musicque vniforme; i'ay bien voulu reseruer ce mien quatrieme diuersifié aux precedents, pour en faire vn arrest & conclusion de mes editions, & le presenter deuant vos S^ries^, comme à vn corps general d'vne des plus louables & fameuses Republiques de toute l'Europe. Vous suppliant, de n'auoir tant d'esgard à la valeur du present, qu'à la prompte volonté & ardeur qu'ay de vous humblement seruir, comme loyal & recognoissant nourriçon de vos liberalitez. Asseurant V. S. que, s'il plaist à icelles d'auoir aggreable ce mien petit labeur, & le prendre soubz leur defense & protection, m'encourageront (& peut estre quelques aultres professeurs de la dite science) de faire quelque aultre œuure, à l'illustration de ceste nostre patrie, de plus grand poids à l'aduenir. Priant en cest endroict le Createur,* MESSEIGNEVRS, *(apres mes treshumbles & tresaffectueuses recommandations à vos bonnes graces) vous octroyer accroissement d'honneurs, & accomplissement de vos nobles & vertueux desirs. D'Anuers, ce* XII. *de Ianuier.* M. D. XCI.

De vos S^ries^ treshumble seruiteur

André Peuernage.

Plate II. André Pevernage: *Livre quatrième des chansons . . .* (1591)
Superius partbook, dedication page.
(Bayerische Staatsbibliothek, Munich)

Plate III. André Pevernage: *Livre quatrième des chansons . . .* (1591)
Superius partbook, opening page of no. 1, *Clio, chantons disertement la gloire.*
(Bayerische Staatsbibliothek, Munich)

LOVANGE DE LA VILLE D'ANVERS.

CLio chantons diſertement la gloire
Et le beau los de la ville d'Anuers,
Faiſons ſon los au temple de memoire,
Viure à iamais par l'ardeur de mes vers.

Du peuple auſſi, & de la Republicque,
Chantons l'honneur, & du noble Senat,
Tant moderé, tant ſage & magnificque,
Qu'il faict beau veoir ſi prudent Magiſtrat.

Chantons encor' des Marchans la trafficque,
Et des denrees l'opulente cheuanche,
Qui de l'Europe, d'Aſie, & de l'Africque
De iour en iour leur vient en abondance.

Les bancqs auſſi, les changes & finances,
Les compaignies par tout ceſt vniuers,
Et les comptoirs, les bourſſes & creances
Me ſeruiront pour matiere à mes vers.

Chantons auſſi l'honneur des belles dames,
Tant richement ornees de douceur,
Et des beautez tant des corps que des ames,
Qu'on ne leur peut donner aſſez d'honneur.

En concluant que ceſte ville riche
Eñ grans treſors, & trafficqu'admirable,
Des bons eſprits eſt la vraye nourrice,
N'ayant à ſoy deſſoubs le ciel ſemblable.

Plate IV. André Pevernage: *Livre quatrième des chansons . . .* (1591)
Penultimate page of the Superius partbook with Jan van der Noot's *Louange de la ville d'Anvers.*
(Bayerische Staatsbibliothek, Munich)

LIVRE QUATRIEME DES CHANSONS . . . (1591)

1. Clio, chantons disertement la gloire

[Jan van der Noot]

10
le beau los, [Et le beau los] de la vil- le d'An- vers,
Et le beau los, Et le beau los de la vil- le d'An- vers, [de la vil-le d'An-
le beau los, [Et le beau los;] Et le beau los de la vil- le d'An- vers, de [la vil-le d'An-
le beau los, [Et le beau los,] Et le beau los de la vil- le d'An- vers, de [la vil-le d'An-
-re Et le beau los, Et le beau los de la vil-le d'An- vers, [de la vil-le d'An-
le beau los, [Et le beau los] de la vil- le d'An- vers,
de [la vil- le d'An-vers,] de [la vil- le d'An-
-vers, de la vil- le d'An-vers,] de la vil- le d'An-
-vers,] de la vil- le d'An- vers, de [la vil- le d'An- vers, de la vil- le d'An-
-vers,] Et le beau los de la vil- le d'An- vers, de [la vil- le d'An-
-vers, de la vil- le d'An-vers,] de la vil- le d'An-
[de la vil- le d'An-vers,] de la vil- le d'An-

15
- vers,] Fai- sons son los, [Fai- sons son los,]
- vers, Fai- sons son los au tem- ple de
- vers,] Fai- sons son los, [Fai-sons son los,] Fai- sons son los au tem- ple de
- vers,] Fai- sons son los, [Fai- sons son los] au tem- ple de
- vers, Fai- sons son los, [Fai- sons son los]
- vers, Fai- sons son los au tem- ple de
au tem- ple de me-moi- re, au tem- ple
me-moi- re, au tem- ple de
me-moi- re, au tem- ple [de me-moi- re,] au tem- ple de
me-moi- re, au [tem- ple de me-moi- re,] au tem- ple
au tem- ple de me-moi- re, au tem- ple
me-moi- re, au tem- ple de

20
de me-moi- re, Vi- vr'à ja-mais par l'ar- deur de mes vers, Vi-
— me-moi- re, Vi- vr'à ja-mais, Vi- vr'à ja- mais, Vi-
me- moi- re, Vi- vr'à ja-mais par l'ar- deur de mes vers, Vi-
de me-moi- re, Vi- vr'à ja-mais par l'ar- deur de mes vers, Vi-vr'à ja- mais
de me-moi- re, Vi- vr'à ja-mais par l'ar- deur de mes vers, Vi-
— me-moi- re, Vi- vr'à ja-mais, [Vi- vr'à ja-mais,]
25
- vr'à ja- mais par l'ar- deur de mes vers, par l'ar-
- vr'à ja- mais par l'ar- deur de mes vers, par l'ar- deur
- vr'à ja- mais par l'ar- deur de mes vers, Vi- - vr'à ja- mais par
par l'ar- deur de mes vers,
- vr'à ja- mais par
par l'ar- deur de mes vers,

- deur de mes vers, Vi- vr'à ja- mais,
de mes vers, par l'ar-deur de mes vers, Vi-
[l'ar- deur de mes vers,] par l'ar- deur de mes vers, Vi-
Vi- vr'à ja- mais par [l'ar- deur de mes vers,] Vi-
l'ar- deur de mes vers, [par l'ar- deur de mes vers,]
par l'ar- deur de mes vers, Vi-
30
[Vi- vr'à ja-mais,] Vi- vr'à ja- mais par l'ar-deur de mes vers.
- vr'à ja-mais, Vi- vr'à ja- mais par l'ar- deur de mes vers.
- vr'à ja- mais, [Vi- vr'à ja-mais,] Vi- vr'à ja-mais par l'ar- deur de mes vers.
- vr'à ja-mais, [Vi- vr'à ja-mais] par l'ar-deur de mes vers.
[Vi- vr'à ja-mais,] Vi- vr'à ja- mais par l'ar-deur de mes vers.
- vr'à ja-mais, [Vi- vr'à ja-mais,] par l'ar- deur de mes vers.

2. Du peupl' aussi

10
Re- pu- bli- que, [et de la Re- pu- bli- que,] et de la Re- pu- bli- que, Chan- tons
et de la Re- pu- bli- que, [et de la Re- pu- bli- que,] et de la Re- pu-
Re- pu- bli- que, [et de la Re- pu- bli- que,] et de la Re- pu- bli-
- bli- que, et de la Re- pu- bli- que, [et de la Re- pu- bli- que,] Chan-tons l'hon-neur,
de la Re- pu- bli- que, [et de la Re- pu- bli- que,] Chan- tons
et de la Re- pu- bli- que, et de la Re- pu- bli- que, Chan-
l'hon- neur, Chan- tons l'hon- neur, et
- bli- que, Chan- tons l'hon- neur, et
- que, Chan- tons l'hon- neur, [Chan- tons l'hon- neur,] et
Chan- tons l'hon- neur, et
l'hon- neur, Chan- - tons l'hon- neur, et
- tons l'hon- neur, Chan- tons l'hon- neur, et

15
_ du no- ble Se- nat, et du no- ble Se- nat, [et___ du no- ble Se- nat,]
_ du no- ble Se- nat, et du no- ble Se- nat, et___ [du no- ble Se- nat,] Tant mo-de-ré,___
_ du no- ble Se- nat, [et du no- ble Se-nat,] et___ du no- ble Se- nat,___ Tant
_ du no- ble Se- nat, et du no- -ble Se- nat, [et___ du no- ble Se- nat,] Tant mo-de-
_ du no- ble Se- nat, et du no- ble Se- nat, et___ [du no- ble Se- nat,] Tant mo-de-ré,___
_ du no- ble Se- nat, et___ du no- ble Se- nat,
20
Tant mo-de- ré,___ [Tant mo- de- ré,]___
Tant mo-de- ré,___
mo-de- ré,___ Tant mo-de- ré,___ [Tant
- ré,___ Tant mo-de- ré,___ [Tant mo-de-
Tant mo-de- ré,___
Tant mo-de- ré,___

tant sa- g'et ma- gni- fi- que,
[Tant mo- de- ré,] tant sa- g'et ma- gni-
mo- de- ré,] tant sa- g'et ma- gni- fi- que, tant sa-
- ré,] tant sa- g'et ma- gni- fi- que, tant [sa- g'et ma- gni-
tant sa- g'et ma- gni-
tant sa- g'et ma- gni- fi- que,
25
tant sa- g'et ma- gni- fi- que, Qu'il faict beau veoir, [Qu'il faict beau veoir,]
- fi- que, Qu'il faict beau veoir, Qu'il faict beau veoir, [Qu'il
- g'et ma- gni- fi- que, Qu'il faict beau veoir, [Qu'il faict beau veoir,] Qu'il faict beau
- fi-que,] tant sa- g'et ma-gni- fi- que, Qu'il faict beau veoir, [Qu'il faict beau veoir,]
- fi- que, Qu'il faict beau veoir,
tant sa- g'et ma- gni- fi- que, Qu'il faict beau

30
— Qu'il faict beau veoir, [Qu'il faict beau veoir] ____ si pru-dent
faict beau veoir,] Qu'il faict beau veoir si pru-dent Ma-gi-strat,
veoir, [Qu'il faict beau veoir] si pru- dent Ma-gi- strat, si pru-dent
Qu'il faict beau veoir, Qu'il [faict beau veoir] si pru-dent Ma- gi- strat, si ___
[Qu'il faict beau veoir] si pru-dent Ma-gi-strat,
veoir, [Qu'il faict beau veoir] si pru-dent
Ma-gi- strat, si ____ pru- dent ____ Ma-gi- strat. ____
si pru-dent Ma-gi- strat, si pru- dent Ma- gi- strat.
Ma-gi- strat, [si pru-dent Ma-gi- strat,] si pru- dent ____ Ma- gi- strat.
— pru-dent Ma-gi- strat, si pru- dent, si ____ pru-dent Ma- gi- strat.
si pru-dent, si pru-dent, si pru- dent Ma-gi- strat.
Ma-gi- strat, si ____ pru-dent, si pru- dent Ma- gi- strat.

3. Chantons aussi l'honneur

ri- che-ment or- né- es, [Tant ri- che-ment or- né- es,] Tant
- ment or- né- es, [Tant ri- che-ment or- né- es,] Tant ri- che-ment or-
Tant ri- che-ment or- né- es, Tant ri- che-ment or- né- es de dou-
- ment or- né- es, [Tant ri- che-ment or- né- es] de dou-ceur,
Tant ri- che-ment or- né- es, Tant [ri- che-ment or-
ri- che-ment or-né- es, Tant ri- che-ment or- né- es de
10
ri- che-ment or- né- es de dou- ceur,
- né- es de dou- ceur, de dou- ceur, [de dou- ceur,] Et
- ceur, [de dou-ceur,] de dou- ceur, Et de
[de dou-ceur,] de dou- ceur, Et de beau- tez,
- né- es] de dou-ceur, [de dou- ceur,]
dou- ceur, de dou- ceur, Et

Et de beau- tez, [Et de beau-tez]
de beau-tez, [Et de beau-tez] tant des
beau- tez, Et de beau- tez tant des corps
Et de beau- tez, Et de beau-tez tant des
Et de beau- tez tant
de beau-tez, [Et de beau-tez] tant des corps
15
tant des corps que des a- mes, tant des corps,
corps que des a- mes, que des a- mes, tant des
que des a- mes, que des a- mes, tant des corps, tant des
corps, tant des corps que des a- mes, tant des corps, tant
des corps que des a- mes, que des a- mes, tant des corps,
que des a- mes, tant des corps que des a-

20
— [tant des corps,] tant des corps que des a- mes, tant des
corps que des a- mes, tant [des corps que des a- mes,]
corps que des a- mes, que des a-
— des corps que des a- mes, tant des corps, tant des corps
tant des corps ——— que des a- mes,
- mes, tant des corps que des a- mes, tant —
corps, tant des corps que des a- mes,
Et de beau-tez tant des corps que des a-
- mes, tant des corps, tant des corps que des a-
que des a- mes, tant [des corps que des a-
tant des corps, ——— tant des corps que des a- mes,
— des corps que des a- -

25
Qu'on ne leur peut don-ner as- sez d'hon- neur,
- mes, Qu'on ne leur peut don- ner as- sez d'hon-neur, Qu'on ne leur peut,
- mes, Qu'on ne leur peut don- - ner as- sez d'hon- neur, Qu'on ne leur
- mes,] Qu'on ne leur peut don-ner as- sez d'hon-
Qu'on ne leur peut don- ner as- sez d'hon-neur, Qu'on ne leur peut don- ner as-
- mes, Qu'on ne leur peut don-ner as- sez d'hon-
Qu'on ne leur peut don-ner as- sez d'hon- neur, Qu'on
Qu'on ne leur peut, Qu'on ne leur peut don- ner as- sez d'hon- neur,
peut, Qu'on ne leur peut don- ner as- sez d'hon-neur, as-sez d'hon- neur, Qu'on ne leur peut don-ner as-
- neur, Qu'on ne leur peut don-ner as- sez d'hon- neur, Qu'on ne leur peut don-
- sez d'hon- neur, Qu'on [ne leur peut,]
- neur, Qu'on ne leur peut don-ner as-

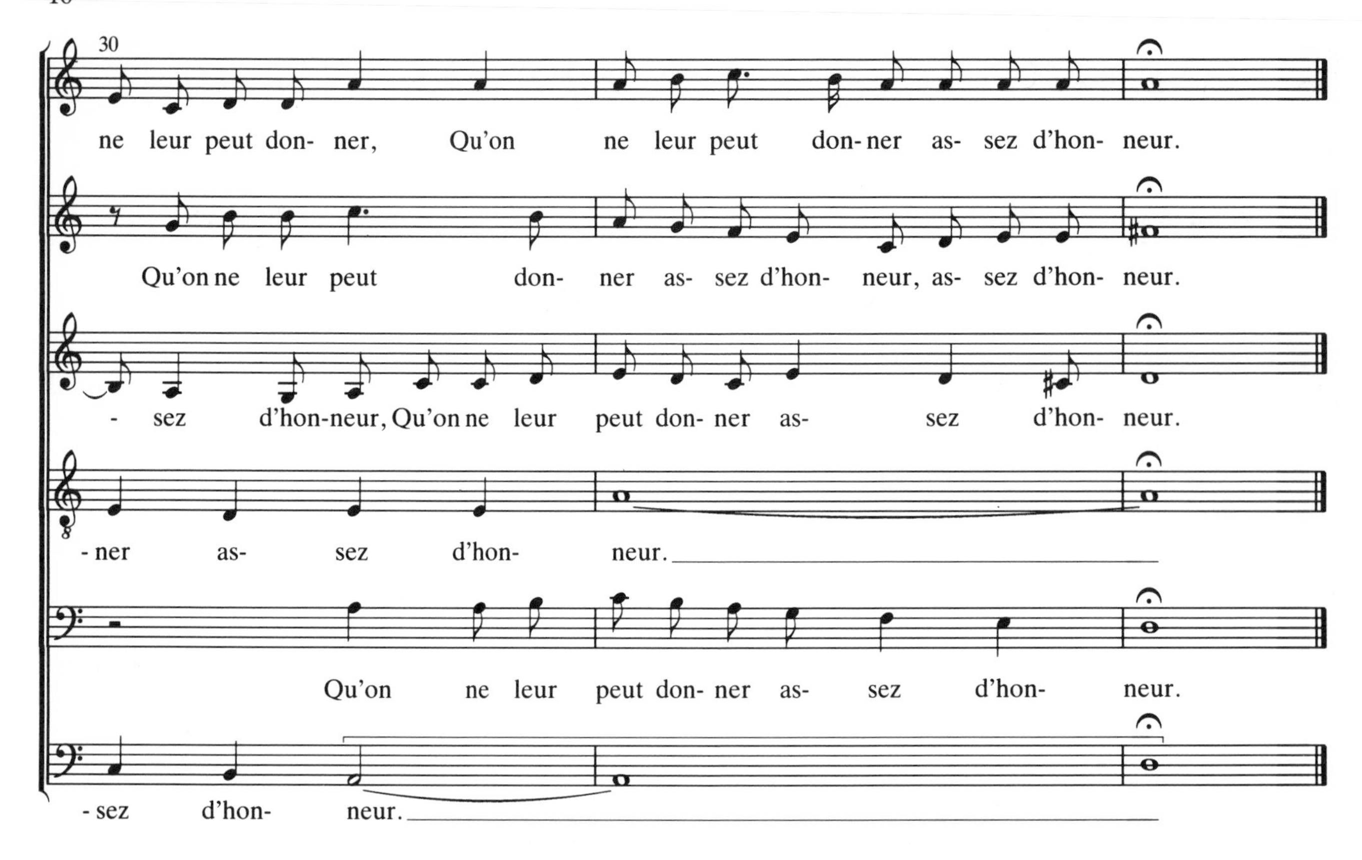

4. Depuis le triste poinct

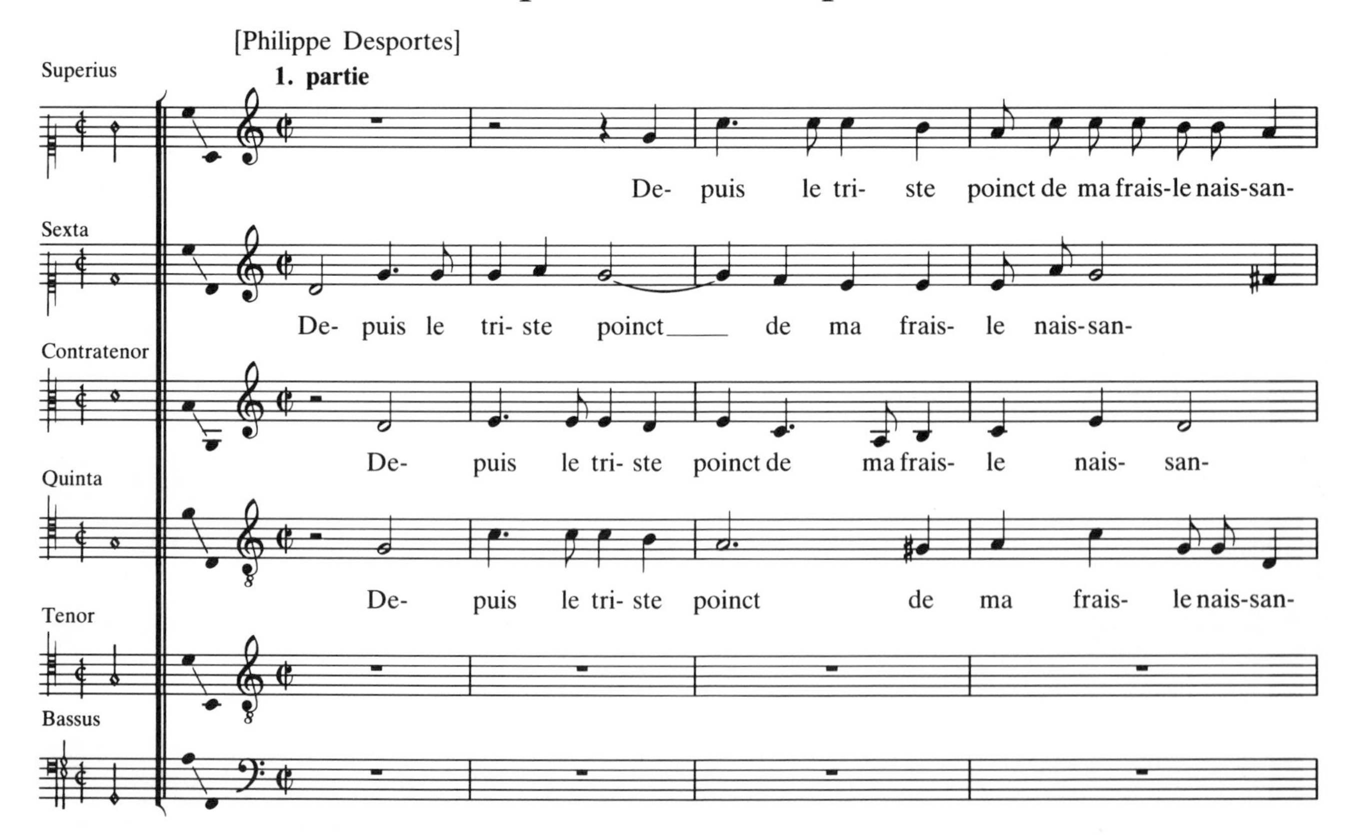

5
- ce, Et que dans le ber-ceau pleu- rant je feu po- sé, Quel jour
- ce, Et que dans le ber- ceau pleu- rant je feu po- sé, Quel jour
- ce, Et que dans le ber-ceau pleu- rant je feu po- sé, Quel jour
- ce, Et que dans le ber- ceau pleu- rant je feu po- sé, Quel
Quel jour mar- qué
Quel jour mar- qué

10
mar- qué de blanc m'a tant fa-vo-ri- sé, Que de l'om- bre d'un bien, Que de l'om-bre d'un
mar- qué de blanc m'a tant fa-vo-ri- sé, Que de l'om-
mar- qué de blanc m'a tant fa- vo- ri- sé, Que de l'om-
jour mar-qué de blanc m'a tant fa-vo-ri- sé, Que de l'om- bre d'un bien
de blanc m'a tant fa-vo-ri- sé, Que de l'om- bre d'un bien j'ay
de blanc m'a tant fa-vo-ri- sé, Que de l'om- bre d'un bien j'ay

15
bien j'ay eu la jou- - is- san- ce? A pei- n'es- toient sei-ché les
- bre d'un bien j'ay eu la jou- is- san- ce?
- bre d'un bien j'ay eu la jou- is- san- ce? A pei- n'es- toient sei-ché les
j'ay eu la jou- is- san- ce?
eu la jou- is- san- ce? A pei-n'es-toient sei- ché les
eu la jou- is- san- ce? A pei- n'es- toient sei-ché les
20
pleurs de mon en-fan- ce, Qu'au froid, au chaud, à l'eau, à l'eau, je
Qu'au froid, au chaud, à l'eau,
pleurs de mon en-fan- ce, Qu'au froid, au chaud, à l'eau, à l'eau, à
Qu'au froid, au chaud, à l'eau, à l'eau, je
pleurs de mon en-fan- ce, Qu'au froid, au chaud, à l'eau,
pleurs de mon en-fan- ce, Qu'au froid, au chaud, à l'eau, à

me vey ex- po- sé D'a- mour, de la fortune,
je me vey ex- po- sé D'a- mour, de la for- tu- ne, D'a-
l'eau, je me vey ex- po- sé D'a-mour, de la for- tu- ne,
me vey ex- po- sé D'a-
à l'eau, je me vey ex- po- sé D'a- mour, de la for- tu- ne, D'a-
l'eau, je me vey ex- po- sé D'a-
25
et des grands mais- tri- sé, Qui m'ont pa-
-mour, de la for- tu- ne, et des grands mais- tri- sé,
et des grands mais- tri- sé, Qui m'ont pa-
-mour, de la for- tu- n',et des grands mais- tri- sé, Qui
-mour, de la for- tu- n',et des grands mais- tri- sé, Qui m'ont pa- yé de
-mour, de la for- tu- ne, et des grands mais- tri- sé,

30
- yé de vent, Qui [m'ont pa- yé de vent,] Qui m'ont pa- yé de
Qui m'ont pa- yé de vent, Qui [m'ont pa- yé de vent,] Qui
- yé, Qui m'ont pa- yé de vent, Qui [m'ont pa- yé de vent,]
m'ont pa- yé de vent, Qui [m'ont pa- yé de vent,] Qui m'ont pa- yé de vent,
vent, Qui m'ont pa- yé, Qui m'ont pa- yé de vent pour tou- te re-com-
Qui m'ont pa- yé de vent, Qui [m'ont pa- yé de vent]
vent, [Qui m'ont pa- yé de vent,] Qui [m'ont pa- yé de vent] pour tou-te
m'ont pa-yé de vent, [Qui m'ont pa- yé de vent] pour tou- te re- com-pen-
Qui m'ont pa- yé de vent, [Qui m'ont pa- yé de vent]___ pour tou- te
Qui [m'ont pa- yé de vent,] Qui m'ont pa- yé de vent, [Qui m'ont pa- yé de
- pen- se, pour tou- te re- com- pen- se, pour [tou- te re-com-pen- se,]
pour tou- te re- com-pen- se, pour [tou- te re- com-pen- se,] pour tou- te

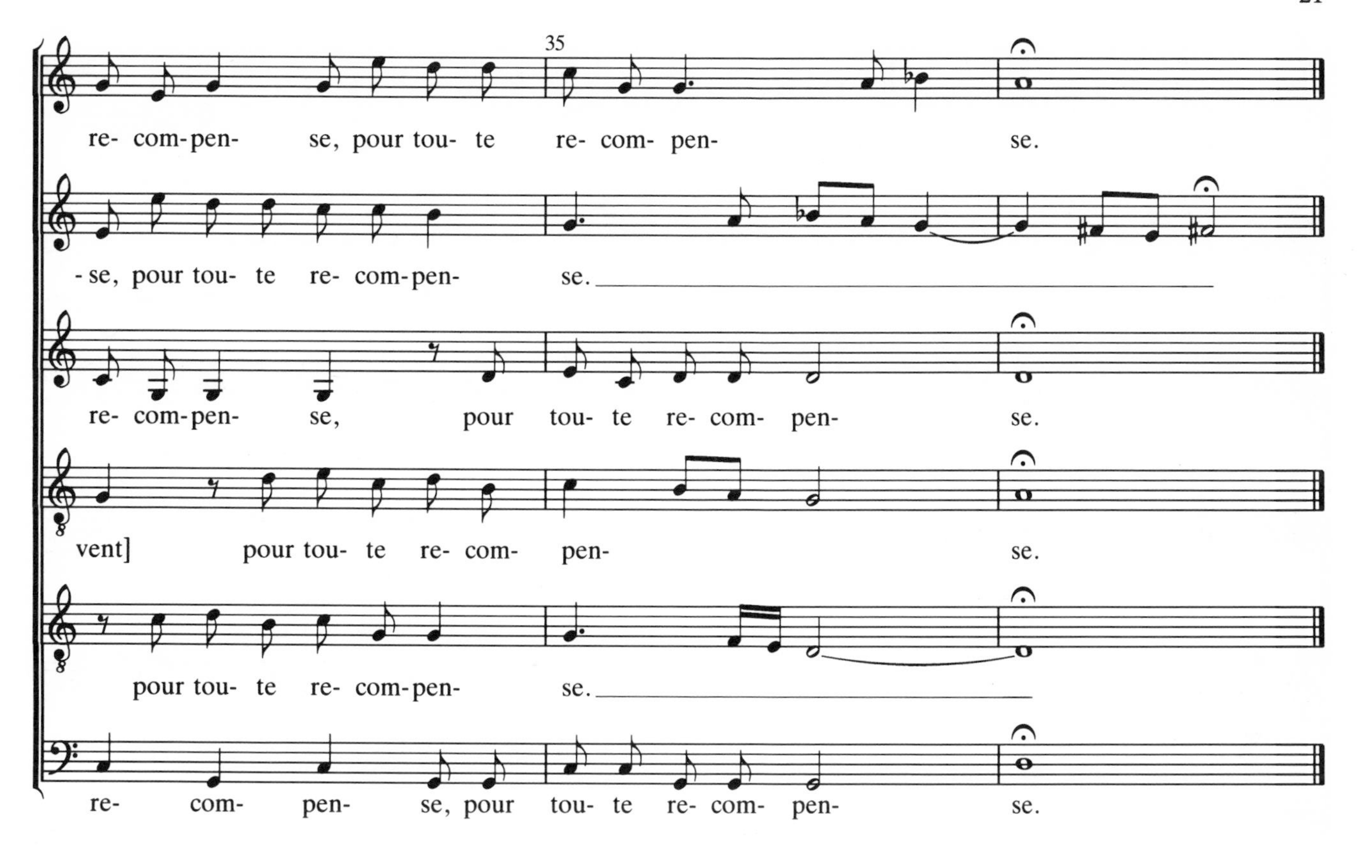

5. J'en suis fable du monde

[Philippe Desportes]

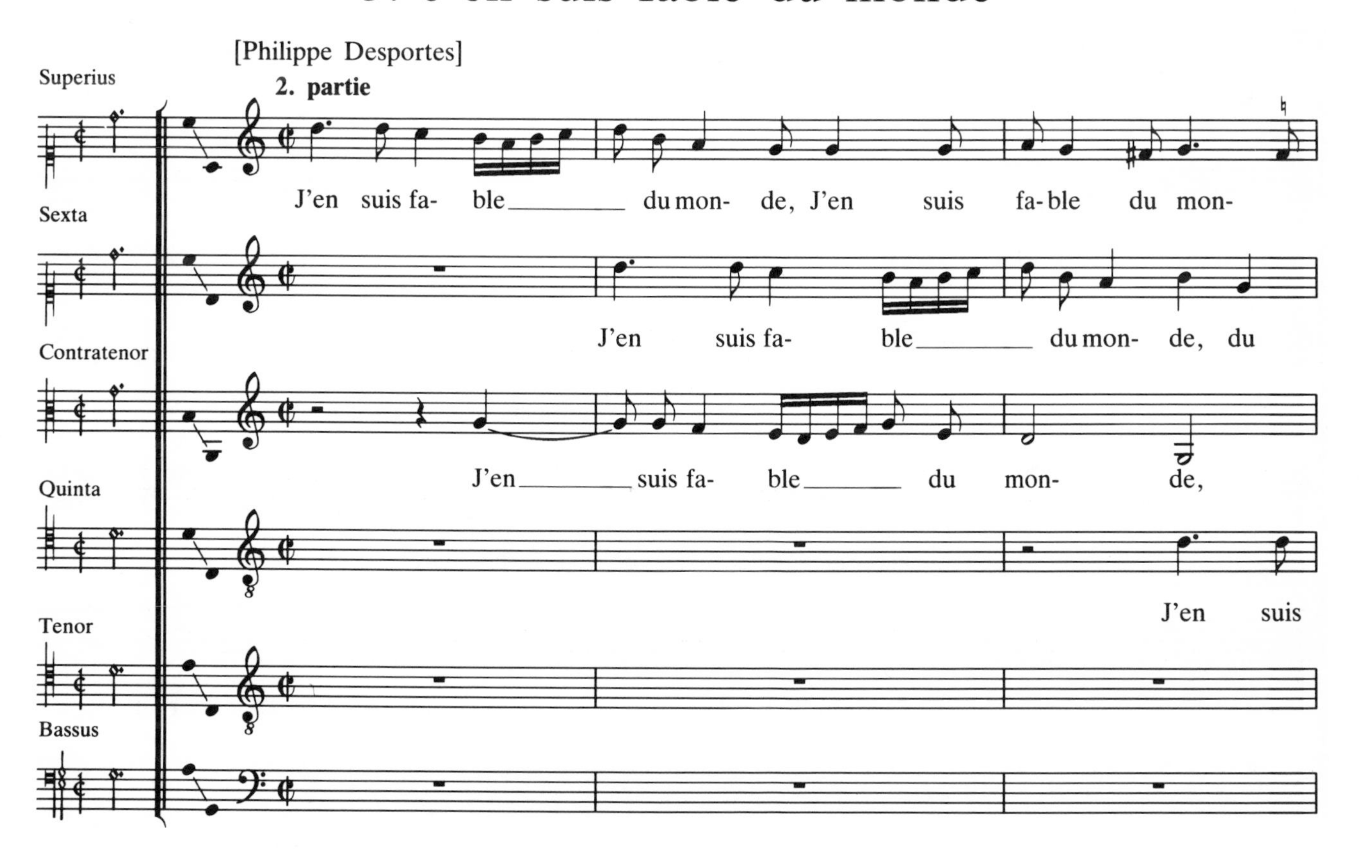

5
- de, et mes vers di- sper- sez
mon- de, et mes vers di- sper- sez
et mes vers di- sper-
fa- ble du mon- de, du mon- de,
J'en suis fa- ble du mon- de,
J'en suis fa- ble du mon- de,
10
Sont les si- gnes pi- teux des maux que j'ay pas- sez,
Sont les si- gnes pi- teux des maux que j'ay pas- sez,
- sez Sont les si- gnes pi- teux des maux que j'ay pas- sez, Quand
Sont les si- gnes pi- teux des maux que j'ay pas- sez, Quand
Sont les si- gnes pi- teux des maux que j'ay pas- sez, Quand tant
Sont les si- gnes pi- teux des maux que j'ay pas- sez, Quand

Quand tant de fiers ty- rans ra- va-
Quand tant de fiers ty- rans ra- va-
tant de fiers ty- rans, Quand tant de fiers ty- rans ra- va-
tant de fiers ty- rans, Quand [tant de fiers ty- rans,]
de fiers ty- rans ra- va-geoyent
tant de fiers ty- rans ra- va-geoyent
15
- geoyent mon cou- ra- - ge: Toy qui m'os-
- geoyent mon cou- ra- - ge: Toy qui m'os-
- geoyent mon cou- ra- ge: Toy qui m'os-
ra- va-geoyent mon cou-ra- ge: Toy qui m'os- tes
mon cou- ra- - ge: Toy qui m'os-
mon cou- ra- - ge: Toy qui m'os-

20
-tes le joug, Toy qui m'os- tes le joug,
-tes le joug, Toy qui m'os- tes le joug, et me fais re- spi-
-tes le joug, Toy [qui m'os- tes le joug,] et me fais re- spi-
le joug, Toy qui m'os- tes le joug, et me fais re- spi-
-tes le joug, Toy qui m'os- tes le joug,
-tes le joug, Toy qui m'os- tes le joug, et me fais re- spi-
25
et me fais re- spi- rer, et me fais re- spi- rer, O Sei- gneur, [O
-rer, et me fais re- spi- rer, O Sei- gneur, [O Sei-
-rer, et me fais re- spi- rer, et [me fais re- spi- rer,] O Sei- gneur, [O
-rer, et me fais re- spi- rer, O Sei- gneur, O
et me fais re- spi- rer, et me fais re- spi- rer, O Sei- gneur,
-rer, et me fais re- spi- rer, O Sei- gneur,

30
_ Sei- gneur,] pour ja-mais vueil- - les moy re- ti- rer De la ter-re d'E-gyp-
- gneur,] pour ja- mais, pour ja-mais vueil- les moy re- ti- rer De la ter-re d'E-gyp-
_ Sei- gneur,] pour ja-mais vueil- les moy re- ti- rer De la ter-re d'E-gyp-
_ Sei- gneur, _ De la ter-re d'E-gyp-
O Sei- gneur,
[O Sei- gneur,]
- te,
- te, pour ja- mais vueil-les moy re- ti- rer De la ter- re d'E-
- te, De la ter- re d'E- gyp- te,
- te, pour ja- mais vueil- les moy re- ti- rer De la ter- re _ d'E-
pour ja- mais vueil- - les moy re- ti- rer _ De la ter- re _ d'E-
pour ja- mais vueil- les moy re- ti- rer De la ter- re d'E-

35
De la ter- re d'E-gyp- te, et d'un si dur ser-
- gyp- te, De [la ter- re d'E-gyp- te,] et d'un si dur ser-
De la ter- re d'E-gyp- te, et d'un si dur ser-
- gyp- te, De la ter- re d'E-gyp- te, et d'un si dur ser- va-
- gyp- te, De la ter- re d'E-gyp- te,
- gyp- te, De la ter- re d'E-gyp- te,
40
- va- ge, et d'un si dur ser- va- ge.
- va- ge, et d'un si dur ser- va- ge.
- va- ge, et d'un si dur ser- va- ge.
- ge, et [d'un si dur ser- va- ge,] et d'un si dur ser- va- ge.
et d'un si dur, et d'un si dur ser- va- ge.
et d'un si dur ser- va- ge.

6. Douce liberté desirée

[Philippe Desportes]

10
-ré- e,
Me lais- sant en cap-ti- vi- té, Me lais-
re- ti- ré- e,
Me lais- sant en cap-ti- vi-té?
re- ti- ré-e,] Me lais- sant en cap-ti- vi- té,
Me
-e, Me lais- -sant en cap-ti- vi- té,
Me lais-
- ti- ré- e,
Me lais- sant en cap-ti- vi- té, Me
-ré- e, Me lais- sant en cap-ti- vi- té,
Me
15
-sant en cap-ti- vi- té? He-las! [He-las!] de moy ne te
He- las! [He- las!] de moy ne te
lais- sant en cap-ti- vi- té? He- las! [He- las!] de moy ne te
- sant en cap-ti- vi- té? He- las! [He- las!]
lais-sant en cap- ti- vi- té? He- las! [He-las!]
lais- sant en cap-ti- vi- té? He- las! [He- las!]

_ des-tour-ne, Re- tour- n'o li- ber- té, Re-tour- n'o
_ des-tour-ne, de moy ne te des-tour- ne, Re-tour- n'o li- ber- té, Re-tour- n'o
_ des-tour-ne, Re-tour- n'o li-ber- té, Re-tour- n'o
de moy ne te des-tour- ne, Re-tour- n'o li-ber-té, Re- tour-
de moy ne te des-tour- ne, Re-tour- n'o li-ber-té, Re-tour-
de moy ne te des-tour- ne, Re-tour- n'o li-ber-té, Re-tour-
20
li- ber- té, re- tour- ne, Re- tour-n'o dou- ce li-ber-té,
li- ber- té, re- tour- ne, re-tour- ne, Re-tour-n'o dou- ce li-ber-té,
li- ber- té, Re-tour- n'o li- ber- té, re-tour- ne, Re-tour-n'o dou- ce li-ber-té,
- n'o li-ber- té, re-tour- ne, re- tour- ne, [re- tour-ne,] Re-
- n'o li-ber- té, re-tour- ne, re- tour- ne, [re- tour-ne,] Re-
- n'o li-ber- té, re- tour- ne, [re- tour- - ne,] Re-

25
Re-tour- n'o dou- ce li-ber- té, re-tour- ne,
Re-tour- n'o dou- ce li- ber- té, re-tour- ne, [re-
Re-tour- n'o dou- ce li- ber- té, re- tour- ne, re-
- tour-n'o dou- ce li-ber-té, Re-tour- n'o dou- ce li-ber-té, re- tour- ne, [re-tour-
- tour-n'o dou- ce li-ber-té, Re-tour-n'o dou- ce li- ber- té, re-tour- ne, [re-
- tour-n'o dou- ce li-ber-té, Re-tour- n'o dou- ce li-ber- té, re-tour- ne,
30
[re-tour- ne, re- tour- ne,] Re-tour- n'o dou- ce li- ber- té.
- tour- ne, re- tour- ne,] Re-tour- n'o dou- ce li- ber- té.
- tour- ne, [re-tour- ne,] Re-tour- n'o dou- ce li- ber- té.
- ne, re-tour- ne,] Re-tour- n'o dou- - ce li- ber- té.
- tour- ne,] Re-tour- n'o dou- ce, Re- tour- n'o dou- ce li- ber- té.
[re-tour- ne,] Re- tour- n'o dou- - ce li- ber- té.

7. Si je vy en peine

10
- gueur,] Si je vy en pei- n'et en lan- gueur,
vy en pei- ne, Si [je vy en pei- ne,] Si je vy en pei- n'et en
en lan- gueur,] Si [je vy en pei- n'et en lan-
Si [je vy en pei- n'et en lan- gueur,] en pei- n'[et en lan-gueur,]
Si je vy en pei- n'et en lan- gueur, [Si je vy
- gueur,] Si [je vy en pei- n'et en lan-gueur,] Si
15
en [lan- - gueur,] De bon gré je le por- te,
lan- gueur, en pei- n'[et en lan- gueur,] De bon gré je le por- te, [De
- gueur,] en pei- n'[et en lan- gueur,] De bon gré je le por- te, [De
Si je vy en pei- n'et en lan- gueur, De bon gré je le por- te,
en pei- n'et en lan- gueur,] De
je vy en pei- n'et en lan- gueur, De

[De bon gré je le por- te,] De [bon gré je le por-
bon gré je le por- te,] De [bon gré je le por- te, De bon gré je le por-
bon gré je le por- te,] De bon gré je le por-
[De bon gré je le por- te,] De [bon gré je le por-
bon gré je le por- te, [De bon gré je le por- te,] je le por- te,
bon gré je le por- te, [De bon gré je le por-
20
- te,] Puis que cel- - le qui a mon coeur, [Puis que
- te,] je le por- te, Puis que cel- le qui a
- te, De [bon gré je le por- te,] Puis que cel- le qui
- te,] Puis que cel- le qui a mon coeur,
Puis que cel- le qui a mon coeur, [Puis que cel- le qui a
- te,] Puis que cel- le qui a

25
cel- le qui a mon coeur,] Puis que cel- le qui a mon coeur, qui [a mon
mon coeur, [Puis que cel- le qui a mon coeur,] Puis [que
a mon coeur, [Puis que cel- le qui a mon coeur,] Puis [que cel-
[Puis que cel- le qui a mon coeur,]
mon coeur,] Puis que cel- le qui a mon
mon coeur, qui [a mon coeur,] Puis que cel- le qui a mon
30
coeur,] Puis [que cel- le qui a mon coeur, Puis que cel- le qui a mon
cel- le qui a mon coeur,] Puis [que cel- le qui a mon coeur,] Puis
-le qui a mon coeur,] Puis que cel- le qui a
Puis que cel- le qui a mon coeur, Puis [que cel- le qui
coeur, Puis que cel- le qui a mon coeur,
coeur, qui a mon coeur, Puis [que

coeur,] Puis [que cel- le qui a mon coeur,]
que cel- le qui a mon coeur, Puis [que cel- le qui
mon coeur, [Puis que cel- le qui a mon coeur,] Puis [que cel- le qui
a mon coeur,] Puis [que cel- le qui a mon coeur,] Puis que cel-
[Puis que cel- le qui a mon coeur,] Puis [que cel- le qui a mon
cel- le qui a mon coeur,] Puis [que cel- le qui a mon
35
qui a mon coeur, Lan- guist de
a mon coeur,] qui a mon coeur, Lan-guist de
a mon coeur,] qui a mon coeur, Lan-guist de
-le qui a mon coeur, qui [a mon coeur,] Lan-guist de
coeur,] qui a mon coeur,
coeur,] Puis que cel- le qui a mon coeur,

40
mes-me sor- te, [Lan- guist de mes-me sor- te,] Lan- guist [de mes-me sor- te, Lan-
mes-me sor- te, Lan- guist de mes-me sor- te,
mes-me sor- te, [Lan- guist de mes-me sor- te,] Lan- guist [de mes-me sor- te,]
mes-me sor- te, [Lan- guist de mes-me sor- te,] Lan-
Lan- guist de mes-me sor- te, [Lan-
Lan- guist de mes-me sor- te, [Lan-
45
- guist de mes-me sor- te,] Lan-guist de mes- me sor- te.
Lan- guist de mes- me sor- te.
Lan- guist de mes- me sor- te.
- guist [de mes-me sor- te,] Lan- guist de mes- - me sor- te.
- guist de mes-me sor- te,] Lan- guist de mes- me sor- te.
- guist de mes-me sor- te,] Lan- guist de mes-me sor- te.

8. La nuict le jour

La nuict [le jour je ne fay que
jour je ne fay que son-ger, La nuict [le jour je ne fay que son-
son- ger,] La nuict le jour je ne fay que
ne fay que son- ger, je ne fay que son- ger: Tout
fay,] je ne fay que son- ger, je [ne fay que son-
son- ger, La nuict le jour je ne fay que son- ger:
10
son- ger:] Tout m'est con- trai- re, [Tout m'est con-trai- re,]
- ger:] Tout m'est con-trai- re, [Tout m'est con- trai- re,] Tout m'est con- trai-
son- ger: Tout m'est con- trai- re, et
m'est con- trai- re, [Tout m'est con- trai- re,] con- trai- re, et
- ger:] Tout m'est con-trai- re, [Tout m'est con-trai-
Tout m'est con- trai- re, [Tout m'est con- trai- re,]

15
et ne puis re- sis- ter, [et ne puis re- sis-
- re, et ne puis re- sis- ter, et [ne puis re- sis-
ne puis re- sis- - ter, et ne puis re- sis- ter:
ne puis re- sis- ter, [et ne puis re- sis- ter:]
- re,] et ne puis re- sis- ter, et [ne puis re- sis-
et ne puis re- sis- ter, et [ne puis re- sis-
- ter:] Le coeur me fault, [Le
- ter:] Le coeur me fault, [Le coeur me
Le coeur me fault, [Le
Le coeur me fault, [Le
- ter:] Le coeur me fault, [Le
- ter:] Le coeur me fault, [Le

20
coeur me fault,] mes e-sprits som- meil- lant Sont a- gi- tez, [Sont a- gi-
fault,] mes e-sprits som- meil- lant Sont a- gi- tez,
coeur me fault,] mes e-sprits som- meil- lant Sont
coeur me fault,] mes e- sprits som- meil- lant Sont a- gi-
coeur me fault,] mes e-sprits som- meil- lant Sont a- gi- tez,
coeur me fault,] mes e-sprits som- meil- lant
25
- tez,] Sont a- gi- tez, [Sont a- gi- tez] com-m'un ruis-seau cou-
[Sont a- gi- tez,] Sont a- gi- tez com- m'un ruis-seau cou- lant,
a- gi- tez, [Sont a- gi- tez,] Sont a- gi- tez com- m'un ruis-seau cou-
- tez, [Sont a- gi- tez,] Sont a- gi- tez, [Sont a- gi- tez] com-
[Sont a- gi- tez,] Sont a- gi- tez, [Sont a- gi- tez]
Sont a- gi- tez, [Sont a- gi- tez,] Sont a- gi- tez com- m'un ruis-

- lant, com- m'un ruis- seau cou- lant, [com- m'un ruis-seau cou-
com- m'un ruis-seau cou- lant, [com- m'un ruis- seau cou-lant,]
- lant, Sont a- gi- tez com- m'un ruis-seau cou- lant, cou- lant, com-
- m'un ruis- seau, com- m'un ruis-seau cou-
com- m'un ruis-seau cou- lant, [com- m'un ruis-seau
- seau cou- lant, [com- m'un ruis-seau cou- lant,] com- m'un ruis-
30
- lant,] com- m'un ruis- seau cou- lant.
com- m'un ruis-seau cou- lant, cou- lant.
- m'un ruis-seau, com- m'un ruis- seau cou- lant.
- lant, com- m'un ruis- seau cou- lant.
cou-lant,] com- m'un ruis-seau cou- lant.
- seau cou- lant, com- m'un ruis-seau cou- lant.

9. Haste le pas et destruy

10
_ dou- leurs; Chas- se ces te- ne- bres, Chas- se
- leurs; ______ Chas- se ces te- ne- bres, Chas- se
ces dou- leurs; Chas- se ces te- ne- bres, Chas- se
de-struy ces dou- leurs; Chas- se ces te- ne- bres, Chas- se
ces dou- leurs; Chas- se ces te- ne- bres, Chas- se
- leurs,] ces dou- leurs, Chas- se ces te- ne- bres, Chas- se
15
[ces te- ne- bres,] ces tra-vaux et lan- gueurs, ____
[ces te- ne- bres,] ces tra-vaux et lan- gueurs, ces ____ tra-vaux et
[ces te- ne- bres,] ces tra-vaux et ______ lan- gueurs,
[ces te- ne- bres,] ces tra-vaux et lan- gueurs, ces ____ tra-vaux et lan-
[ces te- ne- bres,] ces tra- vaux et ________
[ces te- ne- bres,] ces tra-vaux et lan-

20
Ou bien la mort, Ou [bien la mort,] par la fie-
lan- gueurs, Ou bien la mort, [Ou bien la mort,] par la fie- r'A-tro-
Ou bien la mort, [Ou bien la mort,] par la
- gueurs, Ou bien la mort, [Ou bien la mort,] par la fie- r'A- tro-
lan-gueurs, Ou bien la mort, [Ou bien la mort,]
- gueurs, Ou bien la mort, [Ou bien la mort,] par la fie- r'A-tro-
25
- r'A-tro-pos, par [la fie- r'A-tro-pos,] par la fie- r'A- tro- pos, Soit
- pos, par la fie- r'A- tro- pos, Soit a- van- cé, [Soit
fie- r'A- tro- pos, [par la fie- r'A- tro-pos,] Soit
- pos, [par la fie- r'A- tro- pos,] Soit a- van- cé,
par la fie- r'A-tro- pos, par [la fie- r'A- tro- pos,] Soit a- van- cé,
- pos, [par la fie- r'A-tro-pos,] par la fie- r'A-tro-pos, Soit a-van- cé,

30
a- van- cé, [Soit a- van- cé,] si a- vray- je re-pos, [si a- vray- je re- pos,]
a- van- cé,] si a-vray- je re- pos, [si a-vray-
a- van- cé, [Soit a- van- cé,] si a-vray- je re-
[Soit a- van- cé,] si a-vray- je re- pos, si a-
[Soit a- van- cé,] si a-vray- je re-pos, [si
[Soit a- van- cé,] si a- vray- je re-pos,
35
si a- vray- je re-pos, [si a-vray- je re-pos,] si a-vray-je re-
-je re- pos,] si a-vray- je re-pos, [si a- vray- - je re-
-pos, [si a- vray- je re- pos,] si a- vray- je re-
-vray- je, si a- vray- je re-pos, [si a- vray- je re- pos,] si a-vray-je re-
a-vray- je re-pos,] si a-vray- je re- pos, si [a-vray- je re-
[si a-vray- je re- pos,] si a- vray- je re-pos, [si a-vray- je re-

40
-pos, si [a- vray- je re-pos,] si a-vray- je re- pos, [si a-vray-
-pos,] si a- vray- je re- pos, [si a-vray- je re- pos,] si
-pos, [si a-vray- je re- pos,] si [a-vray-
-pos, [si a-vray- je re- pos,] si a- vray- je, si a-
-pos,] si a-vray- je re-pos, si a-vray- je re-pos,
-pos,] si a- vray- je re-pos, [si a-vray- je re-
-je re-pos,] si a- vray- je re-pos, si a- vray-je re- pos.
a- vray- je re-pos, si a- vray- - je re- pos.
-je re- pos,] si a- vray- je re- pos.
-vray- je re-pos, [si a- vray- je re- pos,] si a- vray-je re- pos.
si a- vray- je re- pos, si a- vray- je re- pos.
-pos,] si a- vray- je re-pos, si a- vray- je re- pos.

10. Là où sçavez sans vous

10
cil qui pou-vez sub- ve- nir, qui [pou-vez sub- ve-
es- tes cil qui pou-vez sub- ve- nir
cil, [Vous es- tes cil] qui pou-vez sub- ve- nir, [qui pou-vez sub- ve- nir,] qui pou-vez
cil, [Vous es- tes cil] qui pou-vez sub- ve- nir, qui [pou-vez sub- ve- nir]
es- tes cil qui pou-vez sub- ve- nir, [qui pou- vez sub- ve-
cil qui pou-vez sub- ve- nir, qui [pou-vez sub- ve-
- nir] Fa- ci-le- ment, [Fa- ci- le-ment] à mon cas et af-fai-
Fa- ci-le-ment, [Fa- ci-le-ment] à mon cas et af-fai-
sub- ve- nir Fa-ci- - le-ment à mon cas et af- fai- re, à mon cas et af-fai-
Fa- ci-le- ment, [Fa- ci- le-ment] à mon cas et af- fai- re,
- nir] Fa-ci-le-ment, [Fa- ci- le-ment] à mon cas et af-fai- re, à mon cas et af-fai-
- nir] Fa- ci-le- ment, [Fa- ci-le-ment] à mon cas et af-fai- re,

15
- re, Et des heu-reux, [Et des heu-reux,] Et [des heu- reux,]
- re, Et des heu-reux, [Et des heu-reux,] Et [des heu- reux,]
- re, Et des heu- reux, [Et des heu- reux] de ce mon- de me
Et des heu-reux, Et des heu- reux de ce mon- de me
- re,] Et des heu- reux de ce mon- de me
Et des heu-reux, Et des heu- reux de ce mon- de me
20
Et des heu- reux de ce mon- de me fai- re,
Et des heu- reux de ce mon- de me fai- re, Sans qu'au-
fai- re, Et des heu- reux de ce mon- de me fai- re, Sans
fai- re, Sans qu'au-cun
fai- re, Sans qu'au-
fai- re, Sans

Sans qu'au- cun mal vous en puis- s'ad-ve- nir, vous en puis- s'ad- ve-
- cun mal vous en puis- s'ad- ve- nir, vous en puis-s'ad-ve- nir,
qu'au- cun mal vous en puis- s'ad- ve- nir, vous en puis-
mal vous en puis- s'ad- - ve- nir, Sans qu'au- cun mal vous en puis-s'ad-ve-
- cun mal vous en puis- s'ad- ve- nir, vous en puis-s'ad-ve- nir, Sans
qu'au- cun mal vous en puis- s'ad- - ve- nir,
25
- nir, Sans qu'au- cun mal vous en puis- - s'ad- ve- nir.
Sans qu'au-cun mal vous en puis- s'ad- - ve- nir, vous en puis-s'ad-ve- nir.
- s'ad- ve- nir, vous en puis- s'ad- ve-nir, vous en puis-s'ad- ve- nir.
- nir, Sans qu'au- cun mal vous en puis- s'ad- ve- nir.
qu'au- cun mal vous en puis- s'ad- - ve- nir, vous en puis-s'ad-ve- nir.
Sans qu'au- cun mal vous en puis- s'ad- ve- nir.

11. La belle Marguerite

C'est ___ u- ne no- ble fleur, [C'est ___ u- ne no- ble
u- ne no- ble fleur,] C'est u- ne no- ble fleur,
fleur, [C'est u- ne no- ble fleur, C'est u- ne no- ble
u- ne no- ble fleur,] C'est u- ne no- ble fleur, [C'est u- ne no- ble
C'est u- ne no- ble fleur, [C'est u- ne no- ble
u- ne no- ble fleur,] C'est u- ne no- ble fleur, [C'est u- ne no- ble
15
fleur,] Com- bien qu'el-l'est pe- ti- te, [Com-bien qu'el-l'est pe- ti- te,] Com- bien qu'el-
Com- bien qu'el-l'est pe- ti- te, Com- bien [qu'el-l'est pe-
fleur,] Com-bien qu'el-l'est pe- ti- te, [Com-bien qu'el-l'est pe- ti- te, Com- bien qu'el-
fleur,] Com- bien qu'el-l'est pe- ti- te, Com- bien [qu'el-l'est pe-
fleur,] Com- bien qu'el-l'est pe- ti- te, [Com-bien qu'el-
fleur,] Com- bien qu'el-l'est pe- ti- te, [Com- bien qu'el-

20
- l'est pe-ti- te, El- l'est de grand' va- leur, [El-l'est de grand' va- leur,]
- ti- te,] El- l'est de grand' va- leur, [El-l'est de grand' va-leur,] El- l'est de grand' va-
- l'est pe-ti- te,] El- l'est de grand' va- leur, [El- l'est de grand' va-leur,] El- l'est de grand' va-
- ti- te,] El- l'est de grand' va- leur, [El-
- l'est pe-ti- te,] El- l'est de grand' va- leur, [El- l'est de grand' va-
- l'est pe-ti- te,] El- l'est de grand' va- leur,
25
El- l'est de grand' va- leur.
- leur, [El- l'est de grand' va- leur.] La bel- le
- leur, [El-l'est de grand' va- leur, El- l'est de grand' va- leur.] La bel- le
- l'est de grand' va- leur,] El- l'est de grand' va- leur.
- leur,] El- l'est de grand' va- leur. La bel- le
[El- l'est de grand' va- leur,] El- l'est de grand' va- leur. La bel- le

30
La bel- le Mar- gue- ri- te, [La bel- le Mar- gue- ri-
Mar- gue- ri- te, [La bel- le Mar- gue- ri- te,]
Mar- gue- ri- te, [La bel- le Mar- gue- ri- te,] La [bel- le Mar- gue- ri-
La bel- le Mar- gue- ri- te,
Mar- gue- ri- te, [La bel- le Mar- gue- ri-
Mar- gue- ri- te, [La bel- le Mar- gue- ri-
- te,] C'est u- ne no- ble fleur, [C'est u- ne
C'est u- ne no- ble fleur, [C'est u- ne no- ble fleur,] C'est [u- ne
- te,] C'est u- ne no- ble fleur, [C'est u- ne no- ble fleur,] C'est u- ne
C'est u- ne no- ble fleur, [C'est u- ne
- te,] C'est u- ne no- ble fleur,
- te,] C'est u- ne no- ble fleur,

35
no- ble fleur,] C'est ___ u- ne no- ble fleur, [C'est ___
no- ble fleur,] C'est u- ne no- ble fleur, C'est u- ne no- ble
no- ble fleur, [C'est u- ne no- ble fleur, C'est
no- ble fleur,] C'est u- ne no- ble fleur, [C'est _
[C'est u- ne no- ble fleur,] C'est u- ne no- ble fleur, [C'est
[C'est u- ne no- ble fleur,] C'est u- ne no- ble fleur, [C'est
40
_ u- ne no- ble fleur,] C'est [u-ne no- ble fleur,] C'est ___ u- ne no- ble fleur.
fleur, [C'est u-ne no- ble fleur,] C'est u-ne no- ble fleur. ___
u- ne no- ble fleur,] C'est [u- ne no- ble fleur,] C'est u-ne no- ble fleur.
_ u- ne no- ble fleur,] C'est u- - ne, C'est u- ne no-ble fleur.
u- ne no- ble fleur,] C'est u- ne no- ble fleur. ___
u- ne no- ble fleur,] C'est u- ne no- ble fleur.

12. Le plus grand contentement

C'est de s'es-jou- ir, [C'est de s'es- jou- ir,] C'est de s'es-jou- ir à
C'est de s'es-jou- ir, [C'est de s'es- jou- ir,] C'est de s'es-jou- ir à voir
C'est de s'es-jou- ir, [C'est de s'es- jou- ir] à voir
- ir, [C'est de s'es-jou- ir] à voir, C'est de s'es-jou- ir à
- ir, [C'est de s'es-jou- ir] à voir Cel-
- ir, [C'est de s'es-jou- ir,] C'est de s'es- jou- ir à voir
10
voir Cel- le qui par bon de-voir Scait
Cel- le qui par bon de-voir, Cel- le qui par bon de-voir Scait ver- tu à
Cel- le qui par bon de- voir
voir Cel-le qui par bon de-voir Scait ver-tu à beau-
- le qui par bon de-voir, Cel- le qui par bon de-voir Scait
Cel- le qui par bon de-voir Scait ver- tu à

15
_ ver- tu à beau-té join-dre, Scait ver- tu, ___ Scait ver- tu à
beau-té join-dre, Scait ___ ver- tu à beau-té join- dre, [Scait _
_ Scait ___ ver-tu à beau-té join- dre, à beau-té
- té join-dre, Scait ___ ver- tu à beau- té join- dre, Scait
_ ver- tu à beau-té join-dre, Scait ___ [ver- tu à
beau-té join-dre, Scait ___ ver- tu à beau-té join- dre, [Scait _
20
beau-té join- dre, Scait ___ [ver- tu à beau-té join-
_ ver- tu à beau-té join- dre,] à beau- té join-
join- dre, Scait ver- tu ___ à beau- té join-
ver- tu ___ à beau- té ___ join-
beau-té join- dre,] Scait ___ ver- tu à beau-té join- dre, Fai-
_ ver- tu à beau-té join- dre,] ___

- dre,] Fai-sant à cha- cun sça-voir, Fai-sant à cha- cun sça-voir, [Fai-sant à cha-
- dre, Fai- sant à cha- cun sça-voir, Fai- sant à cha- cun sça-
- dre, Fai- sant à cha-cun sça-voir, Fai- sant [à
- dre, Fai- sant à cha-cun sça-voir, [Fai- sant à cha-
- sant à cha-cun sça-voir, [Fai-sant à cha- cun sça-voir,]
Fai- sant à cha- cun sça-voir, Fai- sant à cha-cun sça-voir,
25
- cun sça-voir,] Fai-sant à cha- cun sça- voir, Que nul ne la peut dis-join- dre,
- voir, à cha- cun sça- voir, Que nul ne la peut dis-join-
cha-cun sça-voir,] Fai-sant à cha-cun sça- voir, Que
- cun sça-voir,] Fai-sant à cha- cun sça-voir, Que nul ne la peut dis-join-
Fai- sant à cha- cun sça-voir, Que nul ne la peut dis-join-
Fai- sant à cha- cun sça- voir, Que

Que nul ne la peut dis- join- dre, [Que nul ne la peut ___ dis-join- dre,]
- dre, Que nul ne la peut ___ dis- join- dre, Que nul ne la peut dis-join- dre, Que
nul ne la peut dis- join- dre, Que [nul ne la peut dis- join- dre,]
- dre, Que nul ne la peut ___ dis- join- dre, ___ dis-join- dre, Que
- dre, Que nul ne la peut dis- join- dre,
nul ne la peut dis- join- dre, ___ Que nul ne
30
Que nul ne la peut, Que nul ne la peut dis- join- dre.
nul ne la peut, Que nul ne la peut dis- join- dre.
Que nul ne la peut dis- join- dre, dis- join- dre.
nul ne la peut dis- join- - dre. ___
Que nul ne la peut ___ dis- join- dre.
la peut dis- join- - dre.

13. O viateur qui par cy passe

10
toy,]
ne vois tu pas ce, [ne
[Ar- res- te toy,]
ne vois tu pas ce, [ne vois tu pas ce,] ne
-res- te toy,]
ne vois tu pas ce, [ne
-res- te toy,]
ne vois tu pas ce, [ne vois tu pas ce,] ne
-res- te toy,]
ne vois tu pas ce, [ne
-res- te toy,]
ne vois tu pas ce, [ne
15
vois tu pas ce,] Que te re- quiert des- ja pas- sé, Que te re- quiert des-
vois tu pas ce, Que te re- quiert des- ja pas- sé, Que te re- quiert des-
vois tu pas ce,] Que te re- quiert des- ja pas- sé,
vois tu pas ce, Que te re- quiert des- ja
vois tu pas ce,] Que te re- quiert des-
vois tu pas ce,] Que te re- quiert des- ja pas- sé,

20
-ja pas- sé, Di- r'au de- funct, Sis
-ja pas- sé, Di- r'au de- funct, [Di- r'au de-funct,] Di- r'au de- funct,
Di- r'au de- funct, [Di- - r'au de-funct,] Di- r'au de- funct,
pas- sé, Di- r'au de- funct, Di- r'au de- funct, [Di- r'au de- funct,]
-ja pas- sé, Di- r'au de- funct, [Di- r'au de- funct,]
Di- r'au de- funct, [Di- r'au de- funct,]
in pa- - ce, Sis in pa- ce.
Sis in pa- ce, Sis in pa- ce.
Sis in pa- ce, Sis in pa- ce.
Sis in pa- ce, Sis in pa- - ce.
Sis in pa- ce, Sis in pa- ce.
Sis in pa- ce, Sis in pa- ce.

14. Ayant couru en diverses provinces

- ses pro- vin- ces,] en [di-ver- ses pro- vin- ces,] en di-
en [di- ver- ses pro- vin- ces,] en di- ver- ses pro-vin- ces, en
- ses pro- vin- ces, Ay- ant cou- ru en di- ver- ses pro- vin- ces, en
- vin- ces,] Ay-ant cou- ru en di-ver- ses pro-vin- ces, en di- ver- ses, en
- ver- ses pro-vin- ces, en [di- ver- ses pro-vin- ces,] en di-ver-
- vin- ces, Ay-ant cou- ru en di-ver- ses
10
- ver- ses pro- vin- - ces, Par mer, par ter- re, [Par mer, par
[di-ver- ses pro- vin- ces,] Par mer, par ter- re, [Par mer, par ter- re,]
[di-ver- ses pro- vin- ces,] Par mer, par ter- re, [Par mer,
di- ver- ses pro- vin- - ces, Par mer, par ter- re, [Par mer, par
- ses pro- vin- ces, Par mer, par ter- re, [Par mer, par
pro- vin- - ces, Par mer, par ter- re, [Par mer, par

15
ter- re,] en po- - ste, [en po-
en po- ste, en [po- st']et
par ter- re,] en po- ste, en
ter- r',]en po- ste, en po- st'et
ter- re,] en po- ste, en po-
ter- re,] en po- ste, en po- st'et
- st']et au- tre- ment, En fur- nis- sant,
au- tre- ment, En fur- nis-
po- st'et au- tre- ment, En fur- nis- sant, [En fur- nis-
au- tre- ment, En fur- nis- sant, [En fur- nis-
- st'et au- tre- ment, En fur- nis-
au- tre- ment, En fur- nis- sant,

20
[En fur- nis- sant] am- bas-sa- des des Prin-ces, En fur- nis- sant am- bas-sa- des des
- sant, [En fur- nis- sant,] En fur- nis- sant am- bas-sa- des des
- sant,] En fur- nis- sant am- bas-sa- des des Prin-ces, En fur-nis- sant am- bas-sa- des des
- sant,] En fur-nis-sant am- bas-sa- des des Prin-ces,
- sant, En fur- nis- sant am- bas-sa- des des
En fur- nis- sant am- bas-sa- des des Prin-ces,
25
Prin- ces, Y con- su- mant du mien
Prin- ces, En fur-nis- sant am- bas- sa- des des Prin- ces, Y con- su- mant du mien
Prin- ces, am- bas- sa- des des Prin-ces, Y con- su- mant du
En fur- nis-sant am- bas- sa- des des Prin- ces,
Prin- ces, En fur- nis- sant am- bas- sa- des des Prin- ces,
En fur- nis- sant am- bas- sa- des des Prin- ces,

30
_ a- bon- dam- ment, Y con-su-mant, Y con- su- mant du
_ a- bon- dam-ment, Y con-su- mant du mien, Y con- su- mant du mien, Y
mien a- bon- dam- ment, du mien a- bon- dam-ment, Y con- su-
Y con- su- mant du mien a- bon- - dam- ment, Y
Y con- su- mant du mien a- bon- dam- ment, Y
Y con-su- mant du mien a- bon- dam- ment,
mien a- bon- dam- ment, Y con- su- mant du mien a- bon- dam- ment.
con- su- mant du mien a- bon- - dam- ment.
- mant du mien a- bon- dam- ment.
con- su- mant, Y con-su- mant du mien a- bon- - dam- ment.
con- su- mant du mien a- bon- dam- ment.
Y con- su- mant du mien a- bon- dam- ment.

15. Retourné suis en ma maison

[Com- ment?] Re- com- pen- sé d'un bel A-
- ment? [Com- ment?] Re- com-pen- sé d'un bel A-
Com- ment?] Re- com- pen- sé d'un bel A-
- ment? [Com- ment?]
- ment? [Com- ment?]
[Com- ment? Com- ment?]
10
- dieu de court, Dont de re-
- dieu de court, Dont de re- gret, [Dont
- dieu de court, Re- com- pen- sé [d'un bel A- dieu de court,] Dont de re- gret,
Re- com- pen- sé d'un bel A- dieu de court, Dont de re-
Re- com- pen- sé d'un bel A- dieu de court,
Re- com- pen- sé d'un bel A- dieu de court, Dont de re-

15
- gret, [Dont de re- gret] qu'on
de re- gret,] Dont de re- gret qu'on
[Dont de re- gret,] Dont de re- gret
- gret, [Dont de re- gret,] Dont de re- gret qu'on
Dont de re- gret qu'on
- gret, [Dont de re- gret]
me tran-choit du sourd, Tout re- ti- ré re- dres-sant
me tran-choit du sourd, qu'on me tran- choit du sourd, Tout re- ti- ré re- dres-sant
qu'on me tran- choit du sourd, Tout re- ti- ré re- dres-sant
me tran-choit du sourd, qu'on me tran- choit du sourd, Tout re- time tran-choit du sourd, Tout re- ti- ré re- dres-sant ma_
qu'on me tran- choit du sourd, Tout

20
ma be-soin- gne, Tout re- ti- ré re- dres-sant ma be- soin- gne, re- dres-
ma be- soin- gne, Tout re- ti- ré re- - dres-sant ma be-
ma be- soin- gne, Tout re- ti- ré re- dres- sant ma be-
- ré re- dres-sant ma be-soin- gne, Tout re- ti- ré re- dres- sant
be-soin- gne, Tout re- ti- ré re- dres-sant ma be-soin- gne, ma
re- ti- ré re- dres-sant ma be- soin- gne, Tout re- ti- ré re- dres-sant
25
- sant [ma be-soin- gne,] Mort, [Mort] m'a sur- pris, qui,
- soin- gne, Mort, [Mort] m'a sur- pris, qui,
- soin- gne, Mort, [Mort] m'a sur-pris, qui,
ma be- soin- gne, Mort, [Mort] m'a sur-pris,
be-soin- gne, Mort, [Mort] m'a sur-pris,
ma be-soin- gne, Mort, [Mort] m'a sur- pris,

30
pour le fai-re court, qui, [pour le fai- re court,] A cy des-sous mis, A cy des-
pour le fai-re court, A cy des- sous mis, A cy [des- sous mis, A cy des-
pour le fai-re court, A cy des-sous mis, A cy des- sous mis, [A
qui, pour le fai-re court, A cy des-sous mis, A cy des-sous,
qui, pour le fai-re court, A cy des-
qui, pour le fai-re court, A cy des- sous mis,
35
- sous, A cy des-sous mis Char- - les de Bour-goin- gne, [Char- les de Bour-
- sous mis,] A cy des- sous mis Char- - les de Bour-goin- gne, [Char- les de Bour-
cy des-sous mis,] A cy des- sous mis Char- les de Bour-goin- gne,
A cy des- sous mis Char- les de Bour- goin- gne, [Char- les de
- sous mis, A cy des- sous mis Char- - les de Bour-goin- gne, [Char- les de Bour-
[A cy des- sous mis] Char- les de Bour- goin- gne,

40
- goin- gne, Char- les de Bour-goin- gne, Char- - les de Bour-goin-gne, Char- les de Bour-goin-
- goin- gne, Char- les de Bour-goin- gne, Char- - les de Bour- goin- - gne,
[Char- les de Bour-goin- gne, Char- - les de Bour-goin-
_ Bour-goin- gne, Char- - les de Bour-goin-gne, Char- les de Bour-goin-
- goin- gne, Char- - les de Bour-goin-gne,
[Char- les de Bour-goin- gne, Char- - les de Bour-goin-gne,
- gne,] Char- les de Bour- goin- gne.
Char- les de Bour-goin- gne,] Char- les de Bour- goin- gne.
- gne,] Char- les de Bour- goin- gne.
- gne, Char- les de Bour-goin- gne,] Char- les de Bour- goin- gne.
Char- les de Bour-goin- gne,] Char- les de Bour- goin- gne.
Char- les de Bour-goin- gne,] Char- les de Bour- goin- gne.

16. Je porte tes couleurs

10
de- mou- rer] tous- jours ton ser- vi- teur, Ne re- fu- se
-rer tous- jours ton ser- - vi- teur, Ne re- fu- se doncq
ton ser- vi- teur, tous- jours [ton ser- vi-teur,] Ne re- fu- se
- mou- rer tous- - jours ton ser- vi- teur, Ne re- fu- se doncq
-rer tous-jours ton ser- vi- teur, Ne re- fu- se doncq
tous-jours ton ser- vi- teur, Ne re- fu- se doncq, Ne re- fu- se
15
doncq point mon mi- se- ra- ble coeur, mon mi- se- ra- ble coeur, Nul au- tre fors que
point mon mi- se- ra- ble coeur, mon mi- se- ra- ble coeur, Nul
doncq point mon mi- se- ra- ble coeur, Nul au-
point mon mi- se- ra- - ble coeur, Nul
point mon mi- se- ra- ble coeur,
doncq point mon mi- se- ra- ble coeur, Nul au- tre

toy luy peut don-ner li- es- se: Et com- m'en
au- tre fors que toy luy peut don- ner li- es- se: Et
- tre fors que toy luy peut don-ner li- es- se:
au- tre fors que toy luy peut don- ner li- es- se: Et
Nul au- tre fors que toy luy peut don- ner li- es- se:
fors que toy luy peut don- ner li- es- se: Et
20
tes cou- leurs, [Et com-m'en tes cou- leurs]
com- m'en tes cou-leurs, [Et com- m'en tes cou-leurs] que por- t'en al- le- gres-
Et com-m'en tes cou- leurs que por- t'en al- le- gres-
com- m'en tes cou-leurs, [Et com-m'en tes cou- leurs] que por- t'en al- le- gres-
Et com-m'en tes cou- leurs
com- m'en tes cou-leurs que por- t'en al- le- gres-

25
que por- t'en al- le-gres- se, Du gris l'on voit qui faict le
- se, que por- t'en al- le- gres- se, Du gris l'on voit qui faict le tra-
- se, Du gris l'on voit qui faict le tra-vail
- se, que por- t'en al- le- gres- se, Du gris l'on voit qui faict
que por- t'en al- le-gres- se, Du gris l'on voit qui faict le tra-
- se, Du gris l'on voit qui faict le tra-vail ou la-
30
tra- vail ou la- beur, Et du blanc, [Et du blanc] qu'est
- vail ou la- beur, Et du blanc, [Et du
ou la- beur, Et du blanc qu'est
le tra-vail ou la- beur, Et du blanc qu'est la foy, [Et
- vail ou la- beur, Et du blanc, [Et du blanc] qu'est
- beur, Et du blanc, [Et du blanc]

la foy, et la jaul- ne cou- leur,
blanc] qu'est la foy, et la jaul- ne cou-leur, La- quel-l'à la bon-heur con-
la foy, et la jaul- ne cou-leur, La- quel-l'à la bon-heur con-
du blanc qu'est la foy,] et la jaul- ne cou-leur,
la foy, La- quel-l'à la bon-heur con-
qu'est la foy, La- quel-l'à la bon-heur con-
35
Ain- si par mon tra-
- ten- te-ment m'ad-dres- se, Ain- - si par mon tra-
- ten- te-ment m'ad- dres- se, Ain- si par mon tra-
Ain- si par mon tra- vail, [Ain-
- ten- te-ment m'ad- dres- se, Ain- si par mon tra-
- ten- te-ment m'ad-dres- se, Ain- si par mon tra- vail,

40
- vail, ma foy, et mon e- spoir, Me- ri- te- ray un jour ta bon-ne gra-c'a-voir, Me-
- vail, ma foy, et mon e-spoir, Me-ri-te- ray un jour ta bon-ne gra-c'a-voir, Me-
- vail, ma foy, et mon e- spoir, Me- ri- te- ray un jour ta bon-ne gra-c'a-voir,
- si par mon tra- vail,] ma foy, et mon e- spoir, Me-
- vail, ma foy, et mon e- spoir, Me- ri-te-
ma foy, et mon e- spoir, Me- ri-te- ray un jour ta bon-ne gra-c'a-voir,
45
- ri- te- ray un jour ta bon- ne gra- c'a- voir, Ou la fie- r'A- tro-
- ri- te- ray un jour ta bon- ne gra- c'a- voir, Ou la fie- r'A-
Ou la fie- r'A- tro-pos met-
- ri- te- ray un jour ta bon- ne gra- c'a- - voir, Ou la fie- r'A-
- ray un jour ta bon- ne gra- c'a- voir, Ou la fie- r'A-
Ou la fie- r'A- tro-pos

50
-pos met- tra fin à ma vi- e:
- tro- pos met- - tra fin à ma vi- e:
- tra fin à ma vi- - e: Tous-jours j'ay bon e-
- tro-pos met- tra fin à ma vi- - e: Tous-jours j'ay bon e-
- tro- pos met- - tra fin à ma vi- e: Tous-jours j'ay bon e-
met- tra fin à ma vi- e: Tous-jours j'ay bon e-
55
Tous- jours j'ay bon e-spoir, Tu
Tous- jours j'ay bon e- spoir, car n'u- sant de ri- gueur,
-spoir, car n'u- sant de ri- gueur,
-spoir, [Tous-jours j'ay bon e- spoir,] car n'u- sant de ri- gueur, Tu
-spoir, [Tous-jours j'ay bon e- spoir,] Tu
-spoir, car n'u- sant de ri- gueur,

m'as vou-lu nom- mer, [Tu m'as vou-lu nom- mer] ton pe-tit ser- vi-
Tu m'as vou-lu nom- mer ton pe-tit ser- vi- teur, Tu [m'as vou-lu nom- mer]
Tu m'as vou-lu nom- mer ton pe-tit ser- vi- teur, Tu m'as vou-lu nom- mer ton pe-tit ser- vi-
m'as vou-lu nom-mer ton pe- tit ser- vi- teur, Tu m'as vou-lu nom- mer ton pe-tit ser- vi-
m'as vou-lu nom-mer ton pe- tit ser- vi- teur,
Tu m'as vou-lu nom- mer, [Tu m'as vou-lu nom- mer] ton pe-tit ser- vi-
60
- teur, Et je te nom-m'aus- si ma mais-tres-
Et je te nom-m'aus- si ma mais-tres-
- teur, Et je te nom-m'aus- si, [Et je te nom-m'aus- si] ma mais-tres-s'et
- teur, Et je te nom-m'aus- si, [Et je te nom-m'aus- si]
Et je te nom-m'aus- si ma mais-tres-
- teur, Et je te nom-m'aus- si

65
-s'et a-mi- e, ma [mais-tres- s'et a- mi- e,]
-s'et a-mi- e, ma [mais-tres-s'et a-mi- e, ma mais-tres- s'et a-mi- e,] ma
a- mi- e, [ma mais-tres-s'et a-mi- e,] ma mais-tres- s'et a- mi- e, [ma mais-
ma mais-tres-s'et a-mi- e, [ma
-s'et a-mi- e, ma [mais-tres- s'et a-mi- e,]
ma mais-tres-s'et a-mi- e, [ma
70
ma [mais-tres- s'et a- mi- e,] ma mais-tres- s'et a-mi- e.
mais-tres-s'et a- mi- e.
-tres- s'et a- mi- e,] ma mais-tres- se et a- mi- e.
mais-tres- s'et a- mi- e,] ma mais- tres- s'et a- mi- e.
ma mais-tres- s'et a- mi- e.
mais-tres- s'et a- mi- e,] ma mais- tres- s'et a- mi- e.

17. Oncques amour ne fut

— sans grand' lan- gueur, sans [grand' lan-
- mour ne fut] sans grand' lan-
· fut sans grand' lan- gueur,] ne fut sans grand' lan-
- gueur,] Onc- ques a- mour ne fut sans grand' lan- gueur,
— ne fut sans grand' lan- gueur,] sans grand' lan-
— sans grand' lan- gueur,
10
- gueur,] Lan-gueur ne fut ja- mais, [Lan-gueur ne fut ja- mais,] Lan- gueur
- gueur, Lan-gueur ne fut ja- mais, [Lan-gueur ne fut ja- mais,] Lan- gueur
- gueur, Lan- gueur ne fut ja- mais, [Lan- gueur
Lan- gueur ne fut ja- mais, Lan- gueur ne
- gueur, Lan- gueur ne fut ja- mais, [Lan-gueur
Lan- gueur ne fut ja- mais, [Lan- gueur

15
ne fut ja-mais sans e- spe- ran- ce, sans [e- spe-ran- ce,] Voi- là le point,
ne fut ja-mais sans e- spe- ran- ce, sans [e- spe-ran- ce,] sans e-
_ ne fut ja-mais] sans e- spe-ran- ce, sans [e- spe-ran- ce,]
fut ja-mais sans e- spe- ran- ce, [sans e- spe-
ne fut ja-mais] sans e- spe- ran- ce, sans e- spe- ran-
ne fut ja-mais] sans e- spe-ran- ce, [sans e- spe-
[Voi-là_ le point, Voi-là_ le point,] Voi- là_ le point,
- spe-ran- ce, Voi-là_ le point, [Voi-là_ le point,]_
Voi- là le point, [Voi- là le point, Voi-là le point,] Voi-là le
- ran- ce,] Voi- là le point, [Voi- là le point,] où
- ce, Voi- là le point, [Voi- là le point,] où gist tout le mal-
- ran- ce,] Voi- là le point, [Voi- là le point,] où

20
où gist tout le mal-heur, où [gist tout le mal- heur,]
où gist tout le mal- heur, Voi- - là le point, où
point, où gist tout
gist tout le mal- heur, où [gist tout le mal- heur,] Voi- là le point,
- heur, tout le mal- heur, où [gist tout le mal- heur,] Voi- là le point, où
gist tout le mal- heur, [où gist tout
25
Qu'on voit sou- vent, [Qu'on voit sou- vent, Qu'on voit sou-
gist [tout le mal-heur,] Qu'on voit sou- vent, [Qu'on voit sou- vent,] Qu'on
le mal- heur, Qu'on voit sou- vent, [Qu'on voit sou-
où gist tout le mal- heur, Qu'on voit sou- vent, [Qu'on voit sou- vent,
gist tout le mal- heur, Qu'on voit sou- vent, [Qu'on
le mal- heur,] Qu'on

- vent, Qu'on voit sou- vent,] Qu'on voit sou- vent,
voit sou- vent, [Qu'on voit sou- vent, Qu'on voit sou- vent,
- vent,] Qu'on voit sou- vent,
Qu'on voit sou- vent,] Qu'on voit sou- vent, [Qu'on
voit sou- vent,] Qu'on voit sou- vent, [Qu'on
voit sou- vent,
[Qu'on voit sou- vent, Qu'on voit sou- vent,] Qu'on
Qu'on voit sou- vent, Qu'on voit sou- vent]
[Qu'on voit sou- vent,] Qu'on voit sou- vent, [Qu'on
voit sou- vent, Qu'on voit sou- vent,]
voit sou- vent, Qu'on voit sou- vent,] Qu'on voit
[Qu'on voit sou-

30
voit sou-vent e- spoir sans jou- is- san- ce, [e- spoir sans jou- is- san- ce,]
— e- spoir sans jou- is- san- ce,
voit sou-vent] e- spoir sans jou- is- san- ce, [e- spoir sans jou- is- san- ce,] e- spoir sans
— e- spoir sans jou- is- san- ce, [e- spoir sans
— sou-vent e- spoir sans jou- is- san- ce, [e- spoir sans
- vent] e- spoir sans jou- is- san- ce, [e- spoir sans
35
e- spoir sans jou- is-san- ce, [e- spoir sans jou-is-san- ce.]
Qu'on voit sou-vent e- spoir sans jou- is-san- ce, e- spoir [sans jou- is- san- ce.]
jou-is-san- ce, [e- spoir sans jou- is-san- ce,] sans jou-is-san- ce.
jou-is-san- ce,] e- spoir sans jou- is- san- ce.
jou-is-san- ce, e- spoir sans jou- is-san- ce,] e- spoir sans jou-is-san- ce.
jou-is-san- ce,] e- spoir sans jou- is- san- ce.

18. Vivre ne puis sur terre

5
Car mort suis à de- my, [Car mort suis à de- my,] Plu-
suis à de- my, Car mort suis à de- my, Car mort suis à de-
Car mort suis à de- my, [Car mort suis à de- my,]
à de- my, Car mort suis à de- my, Car mort suis à de- my, Plu-
Car mort suis à de- my, Car mort suis à de- my,
suis à de- my, Car mort suis à de- my, Plu-
- sieurs me font la quer- - re, [Plu- sieurs me font
- my, Plu- sieurs me font la quer-
Plu-sieurs me font la quer- re, la quer-
- sieurs me font la quer- re, Plu- sieurs me font la quer-
Plu- sieurs me font la quer- re,
- sieurs me font la quer- re, Plu- sieurs me font la

10
— la quer- re,] la quer- re, Et me font en- ne-
- re, Plu-sieurs me font la quer- re, Et me font en- - ne- my, Et
- re, Plu-sieurs [me font la quer- re,] Et me font en- ne- my, Et me font en- ne- my,
- re, la quer- re, Et me font en- ne- my, Et
Plu- sieurs me font la quer- - re, Et me font en- ne-
quer- re, Et me font en- - ne- my, Et
15
- my, Et [me font en- ne-my:] O mort, ve-nez moy quer- re, [O
me font en- ne-my, Et me font en-ne- my: O mort, O mort, ve-nez moy quer-
Et me font en-ne- my: O mort, ve- nez moy quer- re,
me font en- ne-my, Et me font en- ne- my: O mort, ve-nez moy quer- - re, O
- my, Et me font en- ne- my: O mort, ve-nez moy quer-
me font en- ne-my: O mort, ve-nez moy quer- re, O

mort, ve- nez moy quer- re] Sans moy fai- re mer-
- re Sans moy fai- re mer- cy,
O mort, ve- nez moy quer- re Sans moy
mort, ve- nez moy quer- re Sans moy fai- re mer-
- re Sans moy fai- re mer- cy,
mort, ve- nez moy quer- re Sans moy fai- re mer-
20
- cy, O mort, [O mort,] O
Sans moy fai- re mer- cy, O mort, ve- nez moy quer-
fai- re mer- cy, O mort, ve-
- cy, Sans moy fai- re mer- cy, O mort, ve- nez moy quer-
Sans moy fai- re mer- cy, O
- cy, O mort, ve- nez moy quer-

25
mort, ve- nez moy quer- re Sans moy fai- re mer-
- re, O mort, ve- nez moy quer- re Sans
- nez moy quer- re, O mort, ve- nez moy quer-
- re, O mort, ve- nez moy quer- re Sans
mort, ve- nez moy quer- re Sans moy fai- re mer-
- re, O mort, ve- nez moy quer- re Sans
- cy, Sans moy fai- re mer- cy,
moy fai- re mer- cy, [Sans moy fai-
- re Sans moy fai- re mer- cy,
moy fai- re mer- cy, Sans moy fai- re mer- cy, Sans moy
- cy, Sans moy fai- re mer- cy,
moy fai- re mer- cy, Sans moy fai-

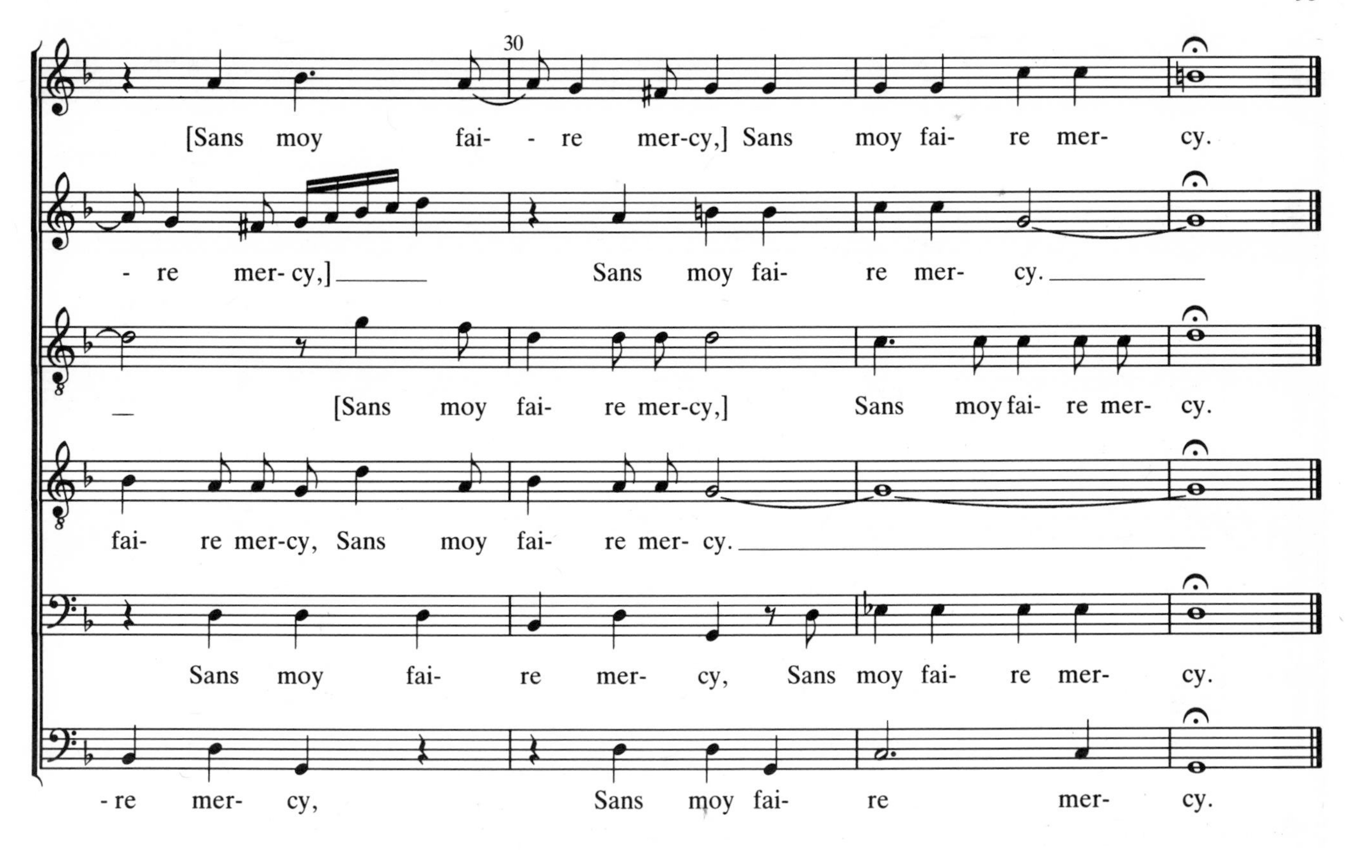

19. Vous perdez temps

5
temps] de me di- re mal d'el- le, de [me di- re mal
de me di- re mal d'el- le, de me di- re mal d'el- le, de me di-
temps] de me di- re mal d'el- le, [de me di- re mal d'el- le,] de [me di-
de me di- re mal d'el- - le,
temps de me di- re mal d'el- le, de me di-
temps de me di- re mal d'el- le, de me di-
10
d'el- le,] Gens qui vou- lez, [Gens qui vou-lez] di- ver- tir
- re mal d'el- le, Gens qui vou-lez, Gens qui vou- lez di- ver- tir mon en- ten-
- re mal d'el-le,] Gens qui vou-lez di- ver- tir, Gens qui vou- lez di-ver-tir mon
Gens qui vou- lez di- ver- tir mon en- ten-
- re mal d'el- le, Gens qui vou-lez, Gens qui vou- lez, Gens qui vou- lez di- ver-tir
- re mal d'el- le, Gens qui vou- lez, Gens qui vou-lez, Gens qui vou- lez di- ver-tir

15
mon en- ten- - te: Plus la bla- mez, [Plus la bla-mez, Plus la bla-mez,] plus
- te: Plus la bla- mez, Plus la bla- mez, Plus la bla- mez, plus
en- ten- - te: Plus la bla- mez, [Plus la bla- mez, Plus la bla-mez,] plus
- te: Plus la bla- mez, Plus la bla- mez,
mon en- ten- te: Plus la bla-mez, Plus la bla- mez, plus
mon en- ten- - te: Plus la bla-mez, Plus la bla- mez,
20
je la trou-ve bel- le, [plus je la trou-ve bel- le;] S'es-ba-hit- on si tant je m'en con-
je la trou-ve bel- le, [plus je la trou-ve bel- le;] S'es-ba-hit- on si tant je m'en con- ten-
je la trou-ve bel- le; S'es-ba-hit- on si tant je m'en con- ten-
plus je la trou- ve bel- le; S'es-ba-hit- on si tant je m'en
je la trou-ve bel- le; S'es-ba-hit- on si tant je m'en
plus je la trou-ve bel- le; S'es-ba-hit- on si tant je m'en con-

25
- ten- te? La fleur de sa jeu-nes- se, A vos-tr'ad-
- te? La fleur de sa jeu-nes- se, A vos-tr'ad- vis rien n'est ce?
- te? La fleur de sa jeu-nes- se, A vos-tr'ad- vis rien n'est ce? N'est
con- ten- te? A vos- tr'ad-vis rien n'est
con- ten- te? La fleur de sa jeu-nes- se,
- ten- te? A vos- tr'ad- vis rien n'est ce?
30
- vis rien n'est ce? N'est ce rien de sa
N'est ce rien de sa gra- ce, [N'est ce rien de sa gra- ce, N'est ce rien de sa
ce rien de sa gra- ce, [N'est ce rien de sa gra- ce,] N'est ce rien de sa
ce? N'est ce rien de sa gra- ce?
N'est ce rien de sa gra- ce?
N'est ce rien de sa gra- ce?

gra- ce? Car mon a-
gra- ce?] Ces- sez voz gran- d'au- da- ce,
gra- ce? Ces- sez voz gran- d'au- da- ce,
Ces- sez voz gran-d'au- da- ce, Car mon a-mour,
Ces- sez voz gran-d'au- da- - ce, Car
Ces- - sez voz gran- - d'au- da- ce,
35
- mour, [Car mon a- mour] vain-cra vos- tre mes- di- re. Tel en mes-dict,
Car mon a- mour, Car mon a-mour vain- cra vos-tre mes- di- - re.
Car mon a- mour vain- cra vos- tre mes- di- re. Tel en mes-dict, [Tel
Car mon a- mour vain-cra vos-tre mes- di- re. Tel en mes-
mon a-mour, Car mon a- mour vain- cra vos-tre mes- di- re.
Car mon a- mour, Car mon a-mour vain- cra vos-tre mes- di- re. Tel

40
[Tel en mes-dict, Tel en mes- dict,] qui
Tel en mes- dict, qui pour soy la de-si- re, qui
en mes- dict, Tel en mes-dict,] qui pour soy la de- si- re, [qui
- dict, Tel en mes- dict, qui pour soy la de-si- re,
Tel en mes-dict, Tel en mes- dict, qui
en mes-dict, Tel en mes-dict, Tel en mes- dict, qui pour soy la de-si- re,
45
pour soy la de-si- re, qui pour soy la de- si- - re.
pour soy la de-si- re, qui pour soy la de- si- re, qui pour soy la de- si- re.
pour soy la de-si- re,] qui pour soy la de- si- re.
qui pour soy la de-si- re.
pour soy la de-si- re, qui pour soy la de- si- re.
qui pour soy la de- si- re.

20. O bien-heureux qui peut passer sa vie

10
- e En- - tre les siens, franc de hai- n'et en- vi-
- e En- tre les siens, franc de hai- - n'et en- vi-
- e En- tre les siens, franc de hai- n'et en- vi-
- e En- tre les siens, franc de hai- n'et en- vi- e, Par-
- tre les siens, En- tre les siens, franc de hai- n'et en- vi-
- e En- tre les siens, franc de hai- n'et en- vi-
15
- e, Par- mi les champs,
- e, Par- mi les champs, Par- mi les champs, les fo- rests
- e, Par- mi les champs, Par- mi les champs, les fo- rests
- mi les champs, Par- mi les champs, les fo-
- e, Par- mi les champs, Par- mi les champs,
- e, Par- mi les champs, Par- mi les champs, les fo- rests

les fo-rests et les bois, les fo-rests et les bois,
et les bois, les fo-rests et les bois, Loing,
et les bois, Par- mi les champs, les fo-rests et les bois, Loing
- rests et les bois, les fo- rests et les bois, Loing
les fo-rests et les bois, les fo-rests et les bois, Loing
et les bois, les fo-rests et les bois, Loing
20
Loing du tu-mul- t'et du bruit po- pu- lai-
Loing du tu-mul- t'et du bruit, Loing du tu- mul- t'et du bruit po- pu-
du tu- mul- t'et du bruit po- pu- lai-
du tu-mul- t'et du bruit, Loing du tu- mul- t'et du bruit po- pu-
du tu-mul- t'et du bruit, Loing du tu-mul- t'et du bruit po- pu-
du tu- mul- t'et du bruit po- pu- lai- re:

25
- re: Et qui ne vend sa li- ber- té pour
- lai- re: Et qui ne vend sa li- ber- té pour plai-
- re: Et qui ne vend sa li- ber- té, Et qui ne vend sa li- ber- té pour plai-
- lai- re: Et qui ne vend sa li- ber- té, sa li- ber- té pour plai-
- lai- re: Et qui ne vend sa li- ber- té pour plai-
Et qui ne vend sa li- ber- té pour plai-
30
plai- re Aux vo- lon- tez, [Aux vo- lon- tez]
- re, pour plai- re Aux vo- lon- tez des
- re Aux vo- lon- tez, [Aux vo- lon- tez] des
- re Aux vo- lon- tez, [Aux vo- lon- tez] des
- re Aux vo- lon- tez des
- re Aux vo- lon- tez, Aux vo- lon- tez

35
des Prin- ces et des Rois, Aux vo- lon- tez des
Prin- ces et des Rois, et ___ des Rois, Aux vo- lon- tez, Aux vo- lon-
Prin- ces et des Rois, des Prin-ces et des Rois, ________ Aux vo- lon- tez des Prin-
Prin- ces et des Rois, des Prin-ces et ________ des Rois, Aux vo- lon-
Prin- ces et des Rois, Aux vo- lon- tez, Aux vo- lon-
des Prin- ces et des Rois, Aux vo- lon- tez des
Prin- ces et des Rois, des Prin- ces et des Rois!
- tez des Prin-ces et des Rois, des Prin- ces et des Rois, des Prin-ces et des Rois!
- ces et des Rois, des Prin- ces et des Rois, des Prin-ces et des Rois!
- tez des Prin-ces et des Rois, des Prin- ces et des Rois, des Prin- ces et des Rois!
- tez des Prin- ces et des Rois, des Prin- ces et des Rois! ________
Prin- ces et des Rois, des Prin- ces et des Rois!

21. Le Rossignol plaisant et gracieux

Aux champs vo- ler, et par tous au- tres lieux, Sa li- ber-
- ler, et par tous au- tres lieux, Sa li- ber- té,
et par tous au- tres lieux, Sa . li- ber- té,
Sa li- ber- té, [Sa li- ber-
Sa li- ber- té, Sa
Sa li- ber- té, Sa
Sa li- ber- té,
10
- té, [Sa li-ber-té] ai- mant mieux que sa ca-
Sa li-ber-té ai- mant mieux que sa ca-
Sa li-ber-té, Sa li-ber-té ai- mant mieux que sa ca- ge:
10
- té] ai-mant mieux que sa ca- ge, Sa li-ber- té ai- mant mieux que sa ca-
li-ber- té ai- mant, Sa li-ber-té ai-mant mieux que sa ca- ge, mieux que sa
li-ber- té ai- - mant mieux que sa ca-
Sa li-ber- té ai- mant mieux que sa ca-

15
- ge: Mais le mien coeur, qui de-meu- r'en os- ta- ge
- ge: Mais le mien coeur, qui de-meu- r'en os- ta- ge
Mais le mien coeur, qui de-meu- r'en os- ta- ge
15
- ge: Mais le mien coeur, qui de-
ca- ge: Mais le mien coeur, qui de-meu- r'en
- ge: Mais le mien coeur, qui
- ge: Mais le mien coeur, qui de-
20
Sous tri- ste dueil,
Sous tri- ste dueil,
Sous tri- - ste dueil,
20
- meu- r'en os- ta- ge Sous
os- ta- ge Sous
de- meu- r'en os- ta- ge Sous
- meu- r'en os- ta- ge Sous tri-

Du Ros-si-
Du
tri- - ste dueil qui le tient en ses lacs,
tri- ste dueil qui le tient, qui le tient en ses lacs,
tri- ste dueil qui le tient en ses lacs, qui le tient en ses lacs,
- ste dueil qui le tient en ses lacs,
25
- gnol, [Du Ros- si- gnol,] Du Ros- - si- gnol ne
Du Ros- si- gnol, Du Ros- si- gnol, Du Ros- si-
Ros- si- gnol ne cer-
25

30
_ cer- che l'a-van-ta- ge, Ne de son chant, [Ne de son chant, _
-gnol ne cer- che l'a-van- ta- ge, Ne de son chant, _ Ne
- che l'a- van-ta- ge, Ne de son chant, _
30
Ne de son chant, _ [Ne de son chant, _
Ne de son chant, _ Ne
Ne de son chant, _ Ne de son
Ne de son chant re- ce- voir le sou-
Ne de son chant, _ Ne de son chant,] _ Ne de son
de son chant, _ Ne de son chant _ re- ce-voir le sou-
_ Ne de son chant, _ Ne
_ Ne de son chant,] _ Ne de son chant _ re- ce-voir, Ne
de son chant, _ Ne de son chant _ re- ce- voir _ le sou-las,
chant re- ce- voir le sou-las, Ne de son chant _ re- ce- voir
-las, Ne de son chant _ re- ce- voir le sou- las, Ne

35
chant, [Ne de son chant, Ne de son chant] re- ce-voir le sou- las,
- las, Ne de son chant re- ce- voir le sou- las, le sou-
de son chant, Ne de son chant re- ce- voir, re-
35
de son chant, [Ne de son chant] re- ce-voir le sou-
Ne de son chant, Ne de son chant re- ce-
le sou- las, Ne de son chant, Ne de son chant, Ne
de son chant re- ce- voir le sou- las, Ne de son
le sou- las, Ne [de son chant,] Ne [de son chant] re- ce-voir le sou- las.
- las, Ne de son chant, Ne de son chant re- ce-voir le sou- las.
- ce-voir le sou-las, Ne de son chant re- ce-voir le sou- las.
- las, Ne de son chant re- ce- voir le sou- las.
- voir le sou- las, Ne de son chant re- ce-voir le sou- las, le sou- las.
de son chant, Ne de son chant re- ce- voir le sou- las.
chant re- ce-voir, re- ce-voir le sou- las, le sou- las.

22. Quand je vous aim' ardentement

10
tou- t'[au-tr'ef- fa- ce,] tou- t'au-tr'ef- fa- ce:
- t'[au-tr'ef-fa- ce,] Vos- tre beau-té tou- t'au-tr'ef- fa- - -
tou- t'au- - tr'ef- fa- ce, [tou-t'au-tr'ef- fa- ce,] tou- t'au-tr'ef-
tou- t'[au-tr'ef- fa- ce,] tou- t'au-tr'ef- fa- -
10
- t'au- tr'ef-fa- ce,] tou- t'au-tr'ef- fa- - -
- t'[au-tr'ef-fa- ce,] tou- t'au- - tre, tou- t'au-tr'ef- fa-
- t'[au-tr'ef-fa- ce,] tou- t'au-tr'ef- fa- ce, [tou- t'au- tr'ef- fa-
15
Quand je vous ai- me froi- - de-ment, Vos-
- ce: Quand je vous ai-me froi-de-ment, Quand [je vous ai-me froi-de-ment,]
- fa- ce: Quand je vous ai-me froi-de-ment, Vos-
- ce: Quand je vous ai- me froi-de-ment, Vos-
15
- ce: Quand je vous ai- me froi- - de- ment,
- ce: Quand je vous ai-me froi-de- ment,
- ce:] Quand je vous ai- me froi-de- ment,

20
- tre beau-té, [Vos- tre beau-té] fond com- - me gla- ce, [fond com-
Vos- tre beau-té, [Vos- tre beau-té] fond com-me gla- ce, fond com- me gla- ce, [fond
- tre beau-té, [Vos- tre beau-té] fond com- me gla- ce, [fond
- tre beau-té, [Vos- tre beau-té] fond com- me gla- ce, [fond
20
Vos- tre beau-té, [Vos-tre beau-té] fond com- -me gla- ce,
Vos- tre beau-té, [Vos-tre beau-té] fond ___ com- me gla- ce,
Vos- tre beau-té, [Vos-tre beau-té] fond com- me gla- ce,
25
-me gla- ce,] Vos- tre beau-té, [Vos- tre beau-té]
com- me gla- ce,] Vos-tre beau-té fond com-me gla- ce, Vos- tre beau-té, Vos- tre beau-té
com- me gla- ce,] Vos- tre beau-té, [Vos- tre beau-té]
com- me gla- ce,] Vos- tre beau-té, [Vos- tre beau-té]
25
[fond com- -me gla- ce,] Vos-tre beau- té, [Vos- tre beau-
[fond com- me gla- ce,] Vos-tre beau- té, [Vos- tre beau-
[fond com- me gla- ce,] Vos-tre beau- té, [Vos- tre beau-

fond com- me gla- ce, [fond com- me gla- ce,]
fond com- me gla- ce, fond [com-me gla- ce,] Vos- tre beau- té fond com- me
fond com- me gla- ce, fond com- me gla- ce,
fond com- me gla- ce, [fond com- me gla- ce,]
- té] fond com- me gla- ce, [fond com- me gla-
- té] fond com- me gla- ce, [fond com- me gla-
- té] fond com- me gla- ce, [fond com- me gla-
30
fond com- me gla- ce, fond com-me gla- - ce.
gla- ce, Vos-tre beau-té, Vos- tre beau- té fond com-me gla- ce.
[fond com-me gla- ce,] fond co- me gla- ce.
fond com-me gla- ce, fond com-me gla- - ce.
30
- ce,] Vos-tre beau- té fond com-me gla- ce, fond com-me gla- ce.
- ce,] fond [com-me gla- ce,] fond com-me gla- - ce.
- ce,] Vos-tre beau- té fond com-me gla- ce.

23. Que ferez-vous, dites ma dame

[Philippe Desportes]

10
N'en au-rez vous plus sou-ve-nan-ce A-pres ce ri-go-reux de- part?
N'en au-rez vous plus sou- ve- nan- ce A-pres ce ri-go-reux de-part?
N'en au- rez vous plus sou-ve-nan-ce A- pres ce ri-go-reux de-part?
N'en au-rez vous plus sou-ve-nan-ce A-pres ce ri- go- reux de- part?
10
- ment. Au
- ment. Au
- ment. Au
- ment. Au
15
De tant d'en-
De tant d'en-nuis qui
De tant d'en-nuis qui
De tant d'en-
15
coeur qui ou-bli' en ab- sen- ce L'a- mour n'a ja-mais eu de part.
coeur qui ou-bli' en ab- sen- ce L'a-mour n'a ja- mais eu de part.
coeur qui ou-bli' en ab- sen- ce L'a-mour n'a ja- mais eu de part.
coeur qui ou-bli' en ab- sen- ce L'a-mour n'a ja-mais eu de part.

-nuis qui vous font guer- re, qui vous font guer-
vous font guer- re, qui vous font guer-
vous font guer- re, qui vous font guer- re
-nuis qui vous font guer- - re, qui vous font guer-
20
- re, Le- quel vous don- ne, Le- quel vous don-ne plus de peur?
-re, Le-quel vous don- ne, Le-quel vous don- ne plus de peur?
Le- quel vous don-ne, Le- quel vous don-ne plus de peur?
- re, Le-quel vous don- ne plus de peur?
20
La crain-te qu'en chan-
La crain-te qu'en chan-
La crain-te qu'en chan-
La crain-te qu'en chan-

25
La crain- te qu'en
La crain- te qu'en
La crain- te qu'en
La crain- te qu'en
25
- geant de ter- re, Il puis-s'aus- si chan- ger de coeur. La crain- te
- geant de ter- re, Il puis-s'aus- si chan- ger de coeur. La crain- te
- geant de ter- re, Il puis-s'aus- si chan- ger de coeur. La crain- te
- geant de ter- re, Il puis-s'aus- si chan- ger de coeur. La crain- te
chan-geant de ter- re, Il puis-s'aus- si chan- ger de coeur.
chan-geant de ter- re, Il puis-s'aus- si chan- ger de
chan-geant de ter- re, Il puis-s'aus- si chan- ger de coeur, chan-
chan-geant de ter- re, Il puis-s'aus- si chan- ger de
qu'en chan-geant de ter- re, Il puis-s'aus- si chan- ger de
qu'en chan-geant de ter- re, Il puis-s'aus- si chan- ger de
qu'en chan-geant de ter- re, Il puis-s'aus- si chan- ger de coeur.
qu'en chan-geant de ter- re, Il puis-s'aus- si chan- ger de

30
— N'u- sez ja- mais de ce lan- ga- ge, de ce lan- ga- ge, A sa foy vous
coeur. N'u- sez ja- mais de ce lan- ga- ge, A sa foy vous
- ger de coeur. N'u-sez ja- mais de ce lan- ga- ge, A sa foy vous
coeur. N'u- sez ja- mais de ce lan- ga- ge, A sa foy vous
30
coeur.
coeur.
—
coeur.
35
faic- tes grand tort.
faic- tes grand tort.
faic- tes grand tort.
faic- tes grand tort.
35
C'est un e- vi-dent te- moi- gna- ge Pour mon-strer, que
C'est un e- vi-dent te- moi- gna- ge Pour mon-strer, Pour mon-
C'est un e- vi-dent te- moi- gna- ge Pour mon- strer, Pour mon-strer, —
C'est un e- vi-dent te- moi- gna- ge Pour mon-strer, Pour mon-

40
Son a-mour si fer- me, si fer-
Son a-mour si fer- m'et si sainc- te
Son a- mour si fer- m'et si sainc- te
Son a-mour si fer- m'et si sainc-
40
j'ai- me bien fort.
- strer, que j'ai- - me bien fort.
que j'ai- me bien fort.
- strer, que j'ai- - me bien fort.
45
- m'et si sainc- te Doit te- nir vos- tr'e- sprit con- tant.
Doit te- nir vos- - tr'e- sprit con- tant.
Doit te- nir vos- tr'e- sprit con- tant.
- te Doit te- nir vos- tr'e- sprit con- tant.
45
Je ne puis que je n'ay- e crain-
Je ne puis que je n'ay- e crain- te De
Je ne puis que je n'a- ye crain-
Je ne puis que je n'ay-e crain- te

De per- dre ce que j'ai-me tant, De
De per- dre, [De per- dre,]
De per-dre ce que j'ai-me tant, De
De per- dre ce que j'ai-me tant, De
-te De per- dre ce que j'ai- me tant, De per-dre ce que j'ai- me
per- dre ce que j'ai- me tant, De per-dre ce que j'ai-me tant,
-te De per- dre ce que j'ai- me tant, De per- dre
De per- dre ce que j'ai- me tant, De [per- dre ce que j'ai-me
50
per- dre ce que j'ai- - me tant.
De per- dre, De per- dre ce que j'ai- me tant.
[per- dre,] De per- dre ce que j'ai- me tant.
[per- dre ce que j'ai-me tant,] De per- dre ce que j'ai-me tant.
50
tant, De per- dre, De per- dre ce que j'ai-me tant.
De per- dre, De per- dre ce que j'ai- me tant.
ce que j'ai-me tant, ce que j'ai-me tant, ce que j'ai- me tant.
tant,] De per- dre ce que j'ai-me tant.

24. Auriez-vous beaucoup de tristesse

10
Quel est le
Quel est le
Quel est le
Quel est le
10
-se Sça- chant bien qu'il n'ai- me que moy.
-se Sça-chant bien qu'il n'ai- me que moy.
-se Sça- chant bien qu'il n'ai- me que moy.
Sça- chant bien qu'il n'ai- me que moy.
mal qui vous of- fen- se, At- ten- dant
mal qui vous of- fen- se, At- ten-dant ce de-
mal qui vous of- fen- se, At- ten-dant ce de- par- te-ment,
mal qui vous of- fen- se, At- - ten-dant ce

15
— ce de- par- te- ment?
-par- te-ment, [At- ten- dant ce de- par- te-ment?]
At- ten- dant ce de- par- te- ment?
— de- par- te- ment?
15
Tel que d'un qui a
Tel___ que d'un
Tel___ que d'un qui
Tel___ que d'un
eu sen- ten- ce Et___ at-
qui a eu sen- ten- - ce Et___ at-
a eu sen- ten- - ce Et at- tend la
qui a eu sen- ten- ce Et at-

20
Quoy? vous pen- sez
Quoy? vous
Quoy? vous
Quoy? vous
20
- tend la mort seu- le- ment.
- tend la mort seu- le- ment.
mort seu- - le- ment.
- tend la mort seu- le- ment.
25
donc- ques à l'heu- re Qu'il s'en i- ra, Qu'il s'en i- ra mou- rir
pen- sez donc- ques à l'heu- re Qu'il s'en i- ra, Qu'il s'en i- ra mou-rir
pen-sez donc-ques à l'heu-re Qu'il s'en i- ra, Qu'il s'en i- ra mou- rir
pen- sez donc- ques à l'heu-re Qu'il s'en i- ra, Qu'il s'en i- ra mou- rir
25

30
d'en- nuy? Il
_ d'en-nuy? Il
_ d'en-nuy? Il
_ d'en-nuy? Il
30
Il ne se peut que je ne meu- re, Mon ___ e-sprit s'en va quant à luy.
Il ne se peut que je ne meu- re, Mon ___ e-sprit s'en va ___ quant à luy.
Il ne se peut que je ne meu- re, Mon ___ e-sprit s'en va quant à luy.
Il ne se peut que je ne meu- re, Mon ___ e-sprit s'en va quant à luy.
35
ne se peut que je ne meu- re, Mon e- sprit s'en va, Mon ___
ne se peut que je ne meu- re, Mon ___ e-sprit s'en va, ___
ne se peut que je ne meu- re, Mon ___ e-sprit s'en va, Mon ___
ne se peut que je ne meu- re, Mon ___ e-sprit s'en va,
35
Il ne se peut que je ne meu- re, Mon e- sprit ___
Il ne se peut que je ne meu- re, Mon e- sprit ___
Il ne se peut que je ne meu- re, Mon e- sprit s'en
Il ne se peut que je ne meu- re, Mon e-

40
_ e-sprit s'en va, Mon_ e-sprit s'en va quant et luy. Si tel ac-ci-dent vous_
Mon e-sprit s'en va, s'en va quant et luy. Si tel ac-ci-dent vous ar-
_ e-sprit s'en va, quant et luy. Si tel ac- ci-dent
Mon e-sprit s'en va quant et luy. Si tel ac-ci-dent vous ar-
40
_ s'en va_ quant et luy._
_ s'en va,_ Mon e- sprit s'en va quant_ et luy.
va, Mon_ e-sprit s'en va quant et luy.
- sprit s'en va, Mon e- sprit s'en va quant et luy.
_ ar- ri- ve, vous ar-ri- ve, Vos- tr'a-mour ne du-re- ra pas, Vos- tr'a-
- ri- ve, vous ar- ri- ve, Vos- tr'a-mour, Vos- tr'a-mour ne
vous ar-ri- ve, vous ar-ri- ve, Vos- tr'a-mour, [Vos- tr'a-mour] ne
- ri- ve, vous ar- ri- ve, Vos- - tr'a-mour, [Vos- - tr'a-mour,] Vos-

45
-mour ne du- re- ra pas.
du- re- ra pas, Vos- tr'a- mour ne du- - re- ra pas.
du- re- ra pas, Vos- - tr'a- mour ne du- re- ra pas.
- tr'a-mour ne du- - re- ra pas.
45
La vray a- mour est
La vray a- mour
La vray a- mour est
La vray a- mour est
50
50
tous- jours vi- ve, La vray a- mour est tous- jours vi-
est tous- jours vi- ve, La vray a- mour est tous-jours vi- ve,
tous- jours vi- ve, La vray a- mour est tous- jours vi-
tous- jours vi- ve, est tous- jours vi-

Et ne meurt point par le tres- pas,
Et ne meurt point par le tres- pas,
Et ne meurt point par le tres- pas,
Et ne meurt point par le tres- pas,
-ve, Et ne meurt point par le tres- pas, Et ne meurt point par le tres-
Et ne meurt point par le tres- pas, Et ne meurt point par le tres-
-ve, Et ne meurt point par le tres- pas, Et ne meurt point par le tres-
-ve, Et ne meurt point par le tres- pas, Et ne meurt point par le tres-
55
Et ne meurt point par le tres- pas, par le tres- pas.
Et ne meurt point par le tres- pas, par le tres- pas.
Et ne meurt point par le tres- pas, Et ne meurt point par le tres- pas.
Et ne meurt point par le tres- pas.
55
-pas, par le tres- pas.
-pas, Et ne meurt point par le tres- pas.
-pas, Et ne meurt point par le tres- pas.
-pas, [Et ne meurt point par le tres- pas.]

25. Soyons plaisans tous gallans

- sans, Soy- ons plai-sans] tous gal- lans, [tous gal-
- sans, Soy- ons plai-sans] tous gal- lans, tous gal-
- sans, [Soy-ons plai-sans] tous gal- lans
- sans, Soy- ons plai-sans] tous gal- lans
- sans] tous gal- lans en de- lais- sant me- lan- co- li-
tous gal- lans en de- lais- sant me- lan- co- li-
tous gal- lans en de- lais- sant me- lan- co- li-
tous gal- lans en de- lais- sant me- lan- co- li-
10
- lans] en de- lais-sant me- lan- co- li- e, Bu- vons d'au- tant, [Bu-
- lans en de- lais-sant me- lan- co- li- e,
Bu-
en de- lais-sant me- lan- co- li- e, en [de- lais-sant me- lan- co- li-
en de- lais-sant me- lan- co- li- e, en [de- lais- sant me- lan- co-
10
- e, tous [gal-lans en de- lais-sant me- lan- co- li-
- e, en [de- lais-sant me- lan- co- li- e,]
- e, en [de- lais-sant me- lan- co- li-
- e, en [de- lais- sant me- lan- co- li-

- vons d'au- tant,] Bu- vons d'au-tant, [Bu- vons d'au- tant, Bu-vons d'au-
- vons d'au-tant, [Bu- vons d'au-tant, Bu- vons d'au-tant,]
- e,] Bu- vons d'au-tant, [Bu- vons d'au-tant,]
- li- e,] Bu- vons d'au-tant, [Bu- vons d'au- tant, Bu- vons d'au-
- e,] Bu-vons d'au-tant, [Bu- vons d'au-tant,] Bu- vons d'au-
Bu- vons d'au-tant, [Bu- vons d'au- tant, Bu- vons d'au-
- e,] Bu-vons d'au-tant, [Bu- vons d'au- tant, Bu- vons d'au-
- e,] Bu-vons d'au-tant, [Bu- vons d'au-tant,] Bu- vons d'au-
15
- tant,] Bu- vons d'au- tant, [Bu-vons d'au- tant, Bu-vons d'au-tant]
Bu- vons d'au- tant, [Bu-vons d'au- tant]
[Bu- vons d'au- tant, Bu- vons d'au-tant]
- tant, Bu- vons d'au- tant]
15
- tant, [Bu-vons d'au- tant, Bu-vons d'au- tant, Bu- vons d'au-tant, Bu- vons d'au-tant, Bu- vons d'au-
- tant, Bu- vons d'au-tant,] Bu- vons d'au-tant, [Bu-vons d'au-
- tant, Bu- vons d'au- tant, Bu- vons d'au-tant, Bu- vons d'au-
- tant, [Bu-vons d'au- tant, Bu- vons d'au-tant, Bu- vons d'au-

20
en me-nant tous-jours vi- e ga- y'et jo- li- e, en me-
en me-nant tous-jours vi- e ga- y'et jo- li- e, en me-
en me-nant tous-jours vi- e ga- y'et jo- li- e,
en me-nant tous-jours vi- e ga- y'et jo- li- e,
20
- tant] en me- nant, [en me-nant] tous- jours vi- e ga-y'et jo- li-
- tant] en me- nant, [en me-nant] tous- jours vi- e ga-y'et jo- li-
- tant] en me- nant tous- jours vi- e ga-y'et jo- li-
- tant] en me- nant tous- jours vi- e ga-y'et jo- li-
25
- nant [tous- jours vi- e ga- y'et jo- li- e.] Lais- sans en- nuy,
- nant tous- jours vi- e ga- y'et jo- li- e. Lais- sans en- nuy,
tous- jours [vi- e ga- y'et jo- li- e.] Lais- sans en- nuy,
tous- jours vi- e ga- y'et jo- li- e. Lais- sans en- nuy,
25
- e, ga- y'et jo- li- e. Lais- sans en- nuy, [Lais-
- e. Lais- sans en- nuy, [Lais-
- e, tous- jours [vi- e ga- y'et jo- li- e.] Lais- sans en- nuy, [Lais-
- e, tous-jours [vi- e ga-y'et jo- li- e.] Lais- sans en- nuy,

Lais- sans en- nuy, pre- nons nos- tre plai- sir,
[Lais-sans en- - nuy,] pre- nons nos-tre plai-sir,
[Lais- sans en- nuy,] pre- nons nos-tre plai-sir,
pre- nons nos-tre plai-sir, [pre-
- sans en- nuy, Lais- sans en- nuy,] pre-
- sans en- nuy,] [Lais- sans en-nuy,] pre-
- sans en- nuy,] pre- nons nos-tre plai-sir, [pre-
Lais- sans en- nuy, pre-
30
[pre-nons nos- tre plai- sir,] Car en la fin
[pre-nons nos- tre plai-sir,] Car en la fin
[pre- nons nos- tre plai- sir,] Car en la fin
- nons nos-tre plai- sir,] pre- nons [nos- tre plai- sir,] Car en la fin
30
- nons nos-tre plai- sir, [pre- nons nos- tre plai- sir,] Car en la fin, [Car en la
- nons nos- tre plai- sir, Car en la fin, [Car en la
- nons nos-tre plai- sir,] pre- nons [nos- tre plai-sir,] Car en la fin, [Car en la
- nons nos-tre plai- sir, Car en la fin, [Car en la

35
le meil- leur nous de-meu- re, le [meil- leur
le meil-leur nous de-meu- re, le meil-leur nous de-
le meil- leur nous de-meu- re, le [meil- leur
le meil- leur nous de-meu- re,
35
fin] le meil- leur nous de-meu- re, [le meil-
fin] le meil-leur nous de-meu- re,
fin] le meil- leur nous de-meu- re,
fin] le meil- leur nous de-meu- re,
40
nous de- meu- re,] Puis qu'il nous faut par- tir,
-meu- re, Puis qu'il nous faut par- tir, [Puis
nous de-meu- re,] Puis qu'il nous faut par- tir, [Puis qu'il nous
Puis qu'il nous faut par- tir, Puis
40
-leur nous de-meu- re,] Puis qu'il nous faut, [Puis qu'il nous
Puis qu'il nous faut par- tir, Puis qu'il
Puis qu'il nous faut par- tir, [Puis qu'il nous faut par-
Puis qu'il nous faut, Puis qu'il nous faut par-

45
[Puis qu'il nous faut par- tir,] Soy- ons plai-
qu'il nous faut par- tir,] Soy- ons plai-
faut par- tir,] Puis [qu'il nous faut par- tir,] Soy- ons plai-
[qu'il nous faut par- tir,] Soy- ons plai-
45
faut par- tir, Puis qu'il nous faut par- tir,]
nous faut par- tir, Puis [qu'il nous faut par- tir,]
- tir,] Puis [qu'il nous faut par- tir,]
- tir, [Puis qu'il nous faut par- tir,]
- sans, [Soy-ons plai-sans] en- co- - re de- my heu-
- sans, [Soy-ons plai-sans] en- co- re de- my heu-
- sans, [Soy-ons plai-sans] en- co- re de- my heu-
- sans, [Soy-ons plai-sans]
Soy- ons plai- sans, [Soy-ons plai- sans] en- co- re
Soy- ons plai- sans, [Soy-ons plai-sans]
Soy- ons plai- sans, [Soy-ons plai-sans]
Soy- ons plai- sans, [Soy-ons plai-sans] en-

50
-re, en- co- re [de-my heu- re, en- co-
-re, [en- co- - re de-my heu- re,
-re, [en- co- re de-my heu- - re,] en-
en- co- re de-my heu- re, [en-
50
de-my heu- re, [en- co- re de-my heu- - re,] en- co-re de-my heu-
en- co- re de-my heu- re, [en- co- re de- my heu-
en- co-re de-my heu- re, en- co-
-co- re de- my heu- re, [en- co- re de-my heu- - re,
55
- re de-my heu- re,] en- co- re de-my heu- re.
en- co- re de-my heu-re,] en- co- re de-my heu- re.
-co- re [de-my heu- re,] en- co- re de-my heu- re.
-co- re de-my heu- re,] en- co- re de-my heu- re.
55
- re.
-re,] en- co- re de- my heu- re.
- re [de-my heu- re,] en- co- re de-my heu- re.
en- co- re de-my heu- re,] en- co- re de-my heu- - re.

26. Bon jour mon coeur

15
jour ma [dou- ce vi- e,] Bon jour mon oeil, [Bon jour ______ mon oeil,] bon
ma dou- ce vi- e,] Bon jour mon oeil, bon jour ma dou- c'a- mi-
bon [jour ma dou-ce vi- e,] Bon jour mon oeil, bon jour, bon jour ma dou- c'a-
dou- ce vi- e, Bon jour mon oeil,
- e,] Bon jour mon oeil, bon [jour ma dou-c'a-
_ ma dou- ce vi- e, Bon jour mon oeil, [bon jour mon oeil,]
Bon jour mon oeil, bon jour ma dou- c'a-
jour ma dou- ce vi- e,] Bon jour mon oeil,
jour ma dou- - c'a- mi- e, bon jour, bon jour ma [dou-
- e, ma [dou-c'a- mi- e,] bon [jour ma dou-
- mi- e, bon [jour ma dou- c'a- - mi- e,] bon jour ma
Bon jour mon oeil, bon jour ma dou-
- mi- e, bon jour ______ ma dou- c'a- mi- e:]
bon jour ma dou- c'a- mi- e, [bon jour ma dou-
- mi- e, bon jour ma [dou- - c'a- mi- e:]
bon jour ma dou- c'a- mi- e, bon jour ma dou-

20
- c'a- mi- e:] Hé bon jour ma tou- te bel- le, Ma mi-
- c'a- mi- e:] Hé bon jour ma tou- te bel- le, Ma
dou-c'a- mi- e: Hé bon jour ma tou- te bel- le, Ma
- c'a- mi- e: Hé bon jour ma tou- te bel- le,
Hé bon jour ma tou- te bel- le, ma [tou-te bel- le,] Ma
- c'a mi- e:] Hé bon jour ma tou- te bel- le,
Hé bon jour ma tou- te bel- le, Ma
- c'a- mi- e: Hé bon jour ma tou- te bel- le,
25
- gnar-di- se, [Ma mi-gnar-di- se, Ma mi-gnar-di- se,] bon jour Mes de- li-
mi-gnar-di- se, [Ma mi- gnar- di- - se,] bon jour Mes de- li-
mi- gnar- di- se, [Ma mi-gnar-di- se,] bon jour Mes de- li-
Ma mi-gnar-di- se, Ma mi-gnar-di- se,
mi- gnar-di- se, bon jour Mes de- li-
Ma mi- gnar-di- se, [Ma mi-gnar-di- se,]
mi-gnar-di- se, [Ma mi-gnar-di- se,]
Ma mi-gnar-di- se,

30
- ces, mon a- mour, Mes [de-
- ces, mon a-mour, bon [jour Mes de- li- - ces, mon a-mour,]
- ces, mon a-mour, Mes
Ma mi-gnar-di- se, bon jour Mes de- li- - ces, mon a- mour,
- ces, mon a- mour, Mes [de-
[Ma mi-gnar-di- se,] bon jour Mes [de- li- - ces, mon a-mour,]
[Ma mi-gnar-di- se,] bon jour Mes de-
Ma mi-gnar-di- se, bon jour Mes de- li- - ces, mon a- mour,
35
- li- ces, mon a- mour.] Mon doux prin-temps, [Mon doux prin-
Mes de- li- ces, mon a- mour. Mon doux prin- temps,
[de- li- ces, mon a-mour.] Mon doux prin-
Mes de- li- ces, mon a- mour. Mon doux prin- temps,
- li- ces, mon a- mour,] mon a- mour. Mon doux prin-temps, [Mon doux prin-
Mes [de- li- ces, mon a- mour.] Mon doux prin-temps,
- li- ces, mon a- mour, [Mes de- li- ces, mon a- mour.] Mon doux prin-
Mes [de- li- ces, mon a- mour.] Mon doux prin- temps,

-temps,] ma dou- ce fleur nou-vel- le, Mon doux plai-
ma dou- ce fleur nou-vel- le, Mon
-temps, ma dou- ce fleur nou-vel- le, Mon doux plai-
ma dou- ce fleur nou-vel- le,
-temps,] ma dou- ce fleur nou-vel- le, Mon doux plai- sir,
ma dou-ce fleur nou-vel- le,
-temps, ma dou- ce fleur nou-vel- le, Mon doux plai-
ma dou- ce fleur nou-vel- le,
40
-sir, ma dou-ce co-lom-bel-le, [ma dou- ce co-lom-bel-le,] ma
doux plai- sir, ma dou- ce, ma dou-ce co-lom-bel- le, ma
-sir, ma dou- ce co-lom-bel-le, ma dou- ce co-lom- bel-
Mon doux plai- sir, ma dou- ce, ma
ma dou-ce co-lom-bel-le, ma [dou- ce co-lom-bel-le,]
Mon doux plai- sir, ma dou- ce co- -lom-bel- le, [ma
-sir, ma dou-ce co-lom-bel-le, ma [dou- ce co-lom-bel-le,] ma
Mon doux plai- sir, ma dou-ce co-lom-bel- le, ma [dou-ce co-lom-

45
[dou- ce co- lom-bel- le,] Mon pas-se- reau, ma gen- te tour- te-rel- le,
[dou- ce co- lom-bel- le,] Mon pas- se- reau, ma gen- te tour-te-rel- le, ma
- le, Mon pas- se-reau, [Mon pas-se- reau,] ___ ma gen-te
dou- ce co- lom-bel- le, Mon pas-se- reau, ma gen-te tour- te- rel- le,
ma [dou-ce co- lom-bel- le,] Mon pas-se- reau, [Mon pas-se- reau,] ma
dou-ce co- lom-bel- le,] Mon pas-se- reau, ma gen- te tour-te-rel- le, ___
dou- ce [co-lom-bel- le,] Mon pas-se- reau, ma
- bel-le,] Mon pas-se- reau,
50
ma [gen-te tour-te- rel- le,] ma [gen- te tour-te-rel- le,] Bon ___ jour ma dou-
[gen- te tour-te-rel- le,] ma [gen- te tour-te-rel- le,] Bon ___ jour ma dou-
gen- te tour-te-rel- le, Bon jour ___ ma dou-ce
ma gen-te tour- te-rel- le, ma gen-te tour- te- rel- le,
gen-te tour- te- rel- le, Bon
— ma gen-te [tour- te- rel- le,]
gen- te tour-te-rel- le, [ma gen- te tour-te-rel- le,]
ma gen- te tour- te- rel- le, Bon ___ jour ma dou-

55
- ce re-bel- le, ma [dou- ce re-bel- le,] Bon jour ma dou- ce re-
- ce re- bel- le, Bon jour ma dou- ce re-
re-bel- le, Bon jour ma dou- ce re- bel-
Bon jour ma dou- ce re- bel- le, ma
jour ma dou-ce re- bel- le, Bon jour ma dou- ce re- bel- le, Bon [jour ma
Bon jour ma dou- ce re-bel- le, [Bon jour ma dou- ce re-
Bon jour ma dou- ce re- bel- le, Bon
- ce re-bel- le, Bon jour, Bon jour ma dou- ce re-bel- le, Bon jour, Bon
60
- bel- le, Bon jour ma dou- ce re-bel- le.
- bel- le, Bon jour ma dou- ce re-bel- le.
- le, ma [dou- ce re- bel- le,] Bon jour ma dou- ce re-bel- le.
dou- ce re- bel- - le.
dou- ce re-bel- le,] Bon jour ma dou- ce re-bel- le.
- bel- le,] ma dou- ce re-bel- le, ma dou- ce re-bel- le.
jour ma dou- ce re- bel- - le.
jour ma dou- ce re- bel- le.

27. Un jour l'amant et l'amie

Orlando [di Lasso]

10
Au beau jeu tant es- prou- vé, A cou- vert Sur
Au beau jeu tant es- prou- vé, A cou-vert
Au beau jeu tant es- prou- vé, A cou-vert Sur
Au beau jeu tant es- prou- vé, A cou-vert Sur le
10
tant es- prou- vé, Au [beau jeu tant es- prou- vé,] A cou-
jeu tant es- prou- vé, Au beau jeu tant es- prou- vé, A cou-
jeu tant es- prou- vé, Au beau jeu tant es- prou- vé, A cou-
jeu tant es- prou- vé, Au beau jeu tant es- prou- vé, A cou-
15
le verd, L'a- mant jou-ait, [L'a-mant jou-ait,] L'a-mant jou- ait
Sur le verd, L'a-mant jou-ait, [L'a-mant jou- ait] par na- tu-
le verd, L'a-mant jou-ait, [L'a-mant jou-ait,] L'a- mant jou- ait
verd, L'a- mant jou-ait, [L'a-mant jou-ait,] L'a- mant jou-ait par
15
- vert Sur le verd, L'a-mant jou-ait, [L'a-mant jou- ait] par na-
- vert Sur le verd, L'a-mant jou-ait, [L'a-mant jou- ait] par na- tu-
- vert Sur le verd, L'a-mant jou-ait, [L'a-mant jou- ait] par na-
- vert Sur le verd, L'a-mant jou-ait, [L'a-mant jou- ait] par na-

20
par na- tu- re, Et l'a- mi- e Sa par- ti- e Te-noit tres-bon-ne me-su-
- re, Et l'a- mi- e Sa par- ti- e Te-noit tres-bon-ne me-su-
— par na-tu- re, Et l'a- mi- e Sa par- ti- e Te-noit tres-bon-ne me-su-
— na- tu- re, Et l'a- mi- e Sa par- ti- e Te-noit tres-bon-ne me-su-
20
- tu- re, Et l'a-mi- e Sa par-ti- e
- re, Et l'a-mi- e Sa par-ti- e
- tu- re, Et l'a-mi- e Sa par-ti- e
- tu- re, Et l'a-mi- e Sa par-ti- e
25
- re. Sous la ver- de cou-ver- tu- re Le Ros-si- gnol j'es-cou-
- re. Sous la ver- de cou-ver- tu- re Le Ros-si- gnol j'es-cou-
- re. Sous la ver- de cou-ver- tu- re Le Ros-si- gnol j'es-cou-
- re. Sous la ver- de cou-ver- tu- re Le Ros-si- gnol j'es-cou-
25
Te- noit tres- bon- ne me- su- re.
Te-noit tres- bon- ne me- su- re.
Te- noit tres- bon- ne me- su- re.
Te-noit tres- bon- ne me- su- re.

30
- tois, Le Pin- son En chan- son
- tois, Le Pin-son En chan- son
- tois, Le Pin- son En chan- son Par
- tois, Le Pin-son En chan-son
Qui chan-toit à l'a-ven-tu- re Là des- sus à hau-te voix. Le Pin-son En chan- son
Qui chan- toit à l'a- ven- tu-re Là des- sus à hau-te voix. Le Pin-son En chan- son
Qui chan- toit à l'a-ven-tu- re Là des- sus à hau-te voix. Le Pin-son En chan-
Qui chan- toit à l'a-ven-tu- re Là des- sus à hau-te voix. Le Pin-son En chan- son
35
Par de-voir fai- soit ho-ma- - ge, La Li- not- te Sur la
Par de- voir fai- soit ho- ma- ge, La Li- not- te Sur la
de-voir fai- soit ho-ma- ge, fai- soit ho- ma- ge, ho-ma- ge, La Li- not- te Sur la
Par de- voir fai- soit ho- ma- ge, La Li- not- te Sur la
Par de- voir fai- soit ho- ma- ge, La Li-not- te
Par de-voir fai- soit ho- ma- - ge, La Li-not- te
- son Par de- voir fai-soit ho- ma- ge, ho-ma- ge, La Li-not- te
Par de- voir fai- soit ho- ma- ge, La Li-not- te

40
mot-te Aux a- mans di- soit cou-ra-ge, cou-ra- ge, [cou- ra- ge,] cou-
mot-te Aux a- mans di- soit cou-ra-ge, cou-ra- ge, [cou-ra- ge,]
mot- te Aux a- mans di- soit cou-ra-ge, cou-ra- ge, [cou-ra- ge,
mot-te Aux a- mans di- soit cou-ra-ge, cou-ra- ge, [cou-ra- ge,] cou-
40
Sur la mot-te Aux a-mans di- soit cou-ra- ge, cou-ra- ge, [cou-ra- ge,] cou- ra-
Sur la mot-te Aux a-mans di- soit cou-ra- ge, cou-ra- ge, cou- ra-
Sur la mot-te Aux a-mans di- soit cou-ra- ge, di- soit cou- ra-
Sur la mot-te Aux a-mans di- soit cou-ra- ge, cou- ra- ge, [cou-ra-
45
- ra- ge, [cou-ra- ge, cou- ra- ge,] cou-ra- ge, cou- ra- ge.
cou- ra- ge, [cou- ra- ge,] cou-ra- ge.
cou- ra- ge,] cou- ra- ge, cou-ra- - ge, [cou-ra- ge,] cou-ra- ge.
- ra- ge, [cou-ra- ge,] cou-ra- ge, [cou-ra- ge,] cou- ra- ge.
45
- ge, [cou-ra- ge, cou- ra- ge,] cou- ra- ge, cou- ra- ge.
- ge, cou- ra- ge, [cou- ra- ge, cou-ra- ge,] cou-ra- ge.
- ge, cou- ra- ge, [cou- ra- ge, cou-ra- ge,] cou-ra- ge.
- ge,] cou- ra- ge, cou-ra- ge, cou- ra- ge.

28. Consecratio mensae

10
- cat dex- te- ra Chri- - sti. In no- mi-ne Pa-tris, et
dex- te- ra Chri- - sti. In no- mi-ne Pa-tris,
be- ne- di- cat dex- te-ra Chri- sti. In no- mi-ne Pa-tris, et
- di- cat dex- te-ra Chri- - sti. In no- mi-ne Pa-tris, In no-mi-ne Pa-tris,
- cat dex- - te-ra Chri- - sti. In no- mi-ne Pa-tris, et
dex- te- ra Chri- sti. In no- mi-ne Pa-tris, et
- di- cat dex- te-ra Chri- sti. In no- mi-ne Pa-tris,
15
Fi- li- i, et Spi- ri- tus, et Spi- ri- tus
et Fi- li- i, et Spi- - ri- tus san-
Fi- li- i, et Fi- li- i, et Spi- ri- tus san- cti. A-
et Fi- li- i, et Spi- ri- tus san-
Fi- li- i, et Spi- ri- tus san- cti, [et
Fi- li- i, et Spi- ri- tus san-
et Fi- li- i, et Spi- ri- tus

20
san- cti, et Spi- - ri- tus san- cti. A-
- cti, et ___ Spi- ri- tus san- cti. A-
- men. et Spi- ri- tus San- cti. A-
- cti, et Spi- ri- tus san- cti. ___
Spi- ri- tus san- cti,] et Spi- ri- tus san- cti. A-
- cti, et Spi- - ri- tus san- cti. A-
san- cti, et Spi- ri- tus san-
25
- men, A- - men, A- - men. ___
- - men, A- men.
- men, ___ A- - men. ___
___ A- - men, A- men.
- men, A- - - men.
- men, A- - men.
- cti. A- - men.

29. Gratiarum actio

10
- ctus in sae-cu- la, sit be-ne-di- ctus in sae- cu-la. A-
- ctus in sae- cu-la, sit be-ne-di- ctus in sae- cu- la.
- ctus in sae- cu-la, sit be-ne-di- ctus in sae-cu- la, sit be- ne- di- ctus in sae- cu-la.
sit be-ne-di- ctus in sae- cu- la, sit be-ne-di- ctus in sae- cu- la. A-
sit be-ne-di- ctus in sae- cu- la, sit be- ne- di- ctus in sae- cu-la. A-
- ctus in sae- cu-la, sit be-ne-di-ctus in sae- cu- la. A-
sit be-ne-di- ctus in sae- cu- la, sit be- ne- di- ctus in sae- cu-la.
15
- men, [A- - men,] A-
A- - men, [A- - men,]
A- - men, A- men, [A-
- men, [A- men,] A-
- men, A- - men, [A-
- men, [A- - men,] A-
A- - men, [A- men,]

- men, [A- -
A- - men, [A-
- men,] A- men, [A-
- men, [A- -
- men, A- men,]
- men, [A- - men,
A- men, [A-
20
- men, A- - men,] A- men.
- men,] A- - men.
- men, A- men,] A- men.
- men,] A- men.
A- - men.
A- - men,] A- men.
- men,] A- - men.

OTHER CHANSONS

[1] Si dessus voz levres de roses

15
- es- ses de- clo- ses, Mon e- sprit, ma vie,
- ses, [Je voy mes li- es- ses] de-clo-ses, Mon e- sprit, ma vie, et mon
voy mes li- es-ses de- clo- - ses,] Mon e-sprit, ma vie, et mon bien, [ma vie, et mon
voy mes li- es- ses] de- clo- ses, Mon e- sprit, ma vie, et mon bien,
20
et mon bien, [ma vie, et mon bien,] ma vie, et mon bien, Vous ne po- vez,
bien, ma vie, et mon bien, [ma vie, et mon bien,] Vous ne po- vez,
bien,] ma vie, et mon bien, [ma vie, et mon bien,] Vous ne po- vez,
ma vie, et mon bien, [ma vie, et mon bien,] Vous ne po-
[Vous ne po- vez] me les de-fen- dre: Par tout, [Par tout, Par
[Vous ne po- vez, Vous ne po-vez] me les de-fen- dre: Par tout, [Par tout,] Par
[Vous ne po-vez] me les de- fen- - dre: Par tout, [Par tout, Par tout,
- vez, [Vous ne po- vez] me les de-fen- dre: Par tout, [Par tout, Par

25
tout] le mien je puis re- pren- dre, [le mien je puis re- pren- dre,] le mien je
tout, [Par tout] le mien je puis re- pren-dre, [le mien je puis re- pren-dre, le mien je
Par tout] le mien je puis re- pren- dre, [le mien je puis re- pren- dre, le mien je
tout,] Par tout le mien je puis re- pren- dre, [Par tout le mien je
30
puis re-pren- dre, Il faut que cha- cun, [Il faut que cha- cun,] Il
puis re- pren-dre,] Il faut que cha-cun, Il faut, [Il faut que cha- cun,]
puis re-pren- dre,] Il faut que cha- cun, Il faut que cha- cun,
puis re-pren- dre,] Il faut que cha- cun, [Il faut que cha- cun, Il
faut que cha- cun ait le sien, Il faut que cha- cun, [Il
Il faut que cha- cun ait le sien, Il faut que cha-cun, cha- cun,
[Il faut que cha- cun] ait le sien, Il faut que cha- cun,
faut que cha- cun] ait le sien, Il faut que cha- cun, [Il

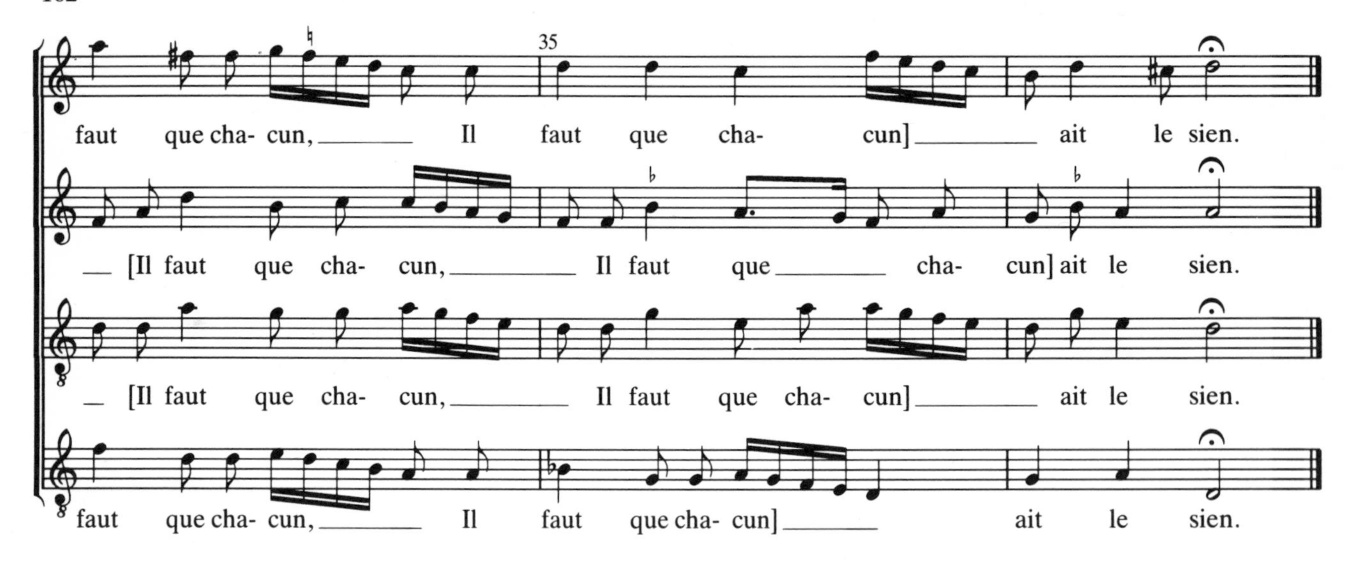

[2] Ma mignonne debonnaire

10
ta- chent qu'à eux com- plai- re, Ne [ta-chent qu'à eux com- plai- - re,] ___
ta- chent qu'à eux com- plai- re, Ne ta- chent, Ne [ta-chent qu'à eux com- plai- re,] Plus
ta- chent qu'à eux com- plai- re, Ne ta- - chent qu'à eux com- plai- re,
ta- chent qu'à eux com- plai- re, [Ne ta- chent qu'à eux com- plai- re,] Plus _
15
— Plus qu'à leurs bel- les a- mours, [Plus qu'à leurs bel- les ___
qu'à leurs bel- - les ________ a- mours, Plus qu'à leurs bel- - les a-
Plus qu'à leurs bel- les a- mours, Plus qu'à leurs bel- les ________
_ qu'à leurs bel- - les a- mours, Plus qu'à leurs bel- - les a-
20
_ a-mours.] Lais-sons les en leur fo- li- e, Et en leur me-lan- co- li- e; Leur _
- mours. Lais- sons les en leur fo- li- e, Et en leur me-lan- co- li- e; Leur a- mi-
_ a- mours. Lais-sons les en leur fo-li- e, Et en leur me- lan-co-li- e; Leur
- mours. Lais-sons les en leur fo- li- e, Et en leur me-lan- co- li- e; Leur

25
_ a- mi- tie ces- se- ra, Leur a- mi- tie ces- - se- ra, Sans fin la
- tie ces-se-ra, [Leur a- mi-tie ces-se- ra,] Leur a- mi- tie ces- - se- ra,
a- mi- tie ces- - se- ra, Leur a- mi- tie ces- se- ra, Sans fin la nos- tre se-
a- mi- tie ces-se- - ra, Leur a- mi- tie ces- - se-ra, Sans fin la
nos- tre se- ra, Sans fin la nos- tre se- ra, Sans fin la nos-
Sans fin la nos- tre se- ra, [Sans fin la nos- tre se- ra,] Sans fin la nos-
- ra, [Sans fin la nos- tre se- ra,] Sans fin la nos- tre se- ra, [Sans fin la
nos- tre se- ra, Sans fin la nos- tre se- ra, [Sans fin la nos- tre se-
30
- tre se- ra, Sans fin la nos- tre se- ra, [Sans fin la nos- tre se-ra.]
- tre se- ra, [Sans fin la nos- tre se- ra,] Sans fin la nos- - tre se- ra.
nos-tre se- ra,] Sans fin la nos- tre se- ra, [Sans fin la nos- tre se-ra.]
- ra,] Sans fin la nos- tre se- ra, [Sans fin la nos- tre se-ra.]

[3] Pour estr' aymé par grande loyauté

10
- té, Car bien sou- vent, [Car bien sou- vent] tant plus la
- de beau- té,] Car bien sou- vent tant plus la
- té, Car bien sou- vent, [Car bien sou- vent, Car bien sou-vent] tant plus la
- té, Car bien sou- vent tant plus la
15
da-me‿est bel- le, [tant plus la da-me‿est bel- le,] tant plus la da-me‿est bel- le, Tant plus el-
da-me‿est bel- le, tant plus la da-me‿est bel- le, [tant plus la da-me‿est bel- le,] Tant plus el-
da-me‿est bel- le, tant plus la da-me‿est bel- le, [tant plus la da-me‿est bel- le,]
da-me‿est bel- le, [tant plus la da-me‿est bel- le,] Tant plus el-
- le‿est, Tant plus el- le‿est à son a- my re- bel- le, [Tant plus el- le‿est à
- le‿est, [Tant plus el- le‿est] à son a- my re- bel- le, Tant plus el- le‿est à
Tant plus el- le‿est à son a- my re- bel- le, [Tant plus el- le‿est à
- le‿est, [Tant plus el- le‿est] à son a- my re- bel- le,

20
son a- my re- bel- le,] Ne luy mon- trant que tou-te cru-au- té, [que
son a- my re- bel- le, Ne luy mon- trant que tou- te cru-au- té,
son a- my re- bel- le,] Ne luy mon-trant que tou-te cru- au-
Ne luy mon- trant que tou-te cru-au- té, [que
25
tou- te cru- au- té,] que tou- te cru- -
que [tou- te cru- au- té,] Ne luy mon- trant, [Ne luy mon-
- té, que [tou- te cru- au- té,] Ne luy mon- trant que tou- te
tou- te cru- au- té,] Ne luy mon- trant, [Ne luy mon-
- au- té.
- trant] que tou- te cru- au- té, [que tou- te cru- au- té.]
cru- au- té, Ne [luy mon-trant que tou- te cru- au- té.]
- trant,] Ne luy mon- trant que tou- te cru- au- té.

[4] Deux que le trait d'Amour

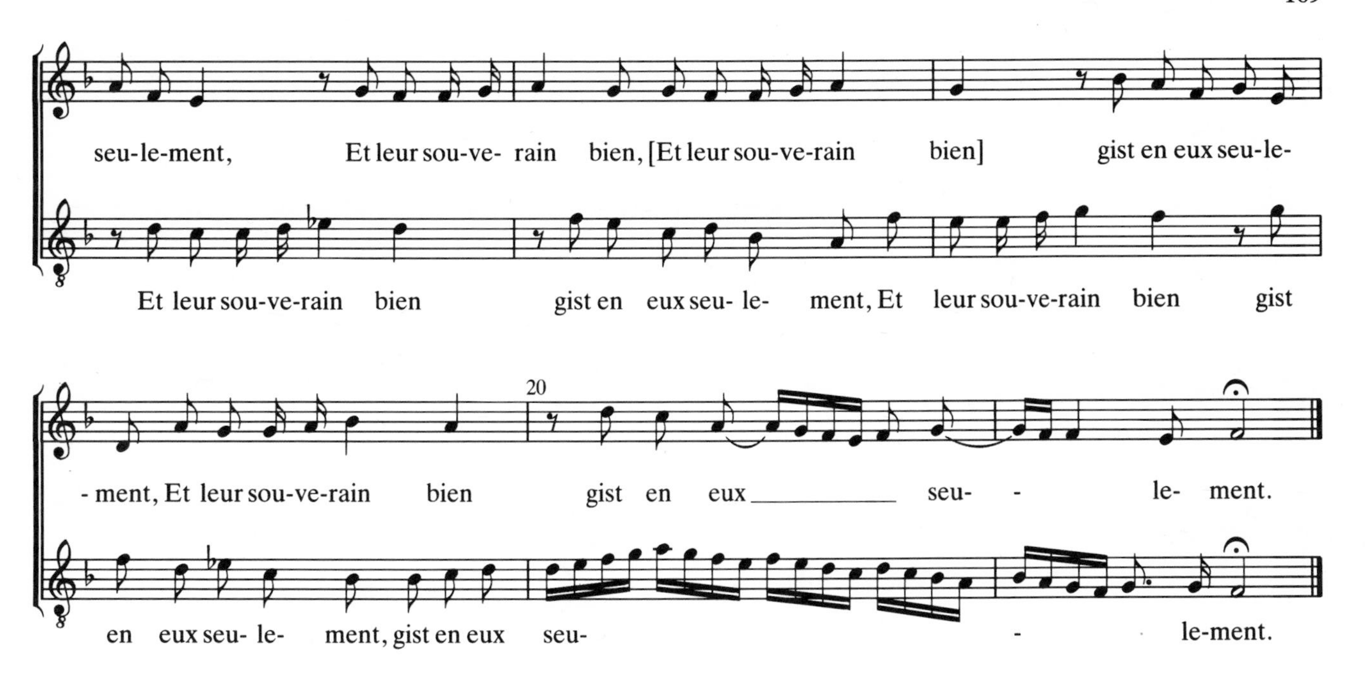

[5] Ilz ont en mesme temps

[Philippe Desportes]

15
[Mesme en- nuy] d'un seul coup, [d'un seul coup] leurs poi- tri- -
ennuy] d'un seul coup, [d'un seul coup] leurs poi- tri- - nes en-
- nes en-ta- - me, Bref leur vie et
20
- ta- - me, Bref leur vie et leur
leur mort pend d'u-ne seu-le tra- me, [pend d'u- ne
25
mort pend d'u- ne seu-le tra- me, [pend d'u-ne
seu-le tra- me] Et com- m'un sim- ple corps, [Et com- m'un sim- ple corps] ilz
seu-le tra-me] Et com- m'un sim- ple corps, [Et com- m'un sim- ple corps] ilz n'ont qu'un
30
n'ont qu'un mou- ve- ment, ilz n'ont qu'un mou-ve-ment, [ilz n'ont qu'un mou- ve- ment,]
mou-ve-ment, ilz n'ont qu'un mou-ve- ment, [ilz n'ont qu'un mou- ve- ment,] ilz n'ont qu'un mou-ve-
35
ilz n'ont qu'un mou-ve-ment, [ilz n'ont qu'un mou-ve-ment,] ilz n'ont qu'un mou- ve- ment.
- ment, [ilz n'ont qu'un mou-ve-ment,] ilz n'ont qu'un mou- ve- ment.

[6] Cest amour qui si rare

[Philippe Desportes]

-vi- se et qui se plaist au chan- - ge N'est
se de- vi- se et qui se plaist au chan- ge
20
point tou-ché d'a- mour, [N'est point tou-ché d'a- mour,] mais
N'est point tou-ché d'a- mour, [N'est point tou- ché d'a- mour,]
25
d'un sa- le plai-sir, [mais d'un sa- le plai- sir,] mais d'un sa- le plai-sir, [mais d'un
mais d'un sa- le plai- sir, [mais d'un sa- le plai-sir,] mais d'un sa- le plai-sir, [mais
sa- le plai-sir,] N'est point tou-ché d'a- mour, [N'est point tou-ché d'a-
d'un sa- le plai-sir,] N'est point tou-ché d'a- mour, [N'est point tou-
30
- mour,] mais d'un sa- le plai-sir, [mais d'un sa- le plai- sir,] mais d'un sa-
- ché d'a- mour,] mais d'un sa- le plai- sir, [mais d'un sa- le plai-sir,] mais d'un
35
- le plai-sir, [mais d'un sa- le plai-sir,] mais d'un sa- le plai- sir.
sa- le plai-sir, [mais d'un sa- le plai-sir,] mais d'un sa- le plai- sir.